THE PURSUIT

A Novella
Mind Sweeper Series Book 4

AE JONES

AE Jones: The Pursuit
Copyright © 2015 by Amy E Jones

AE Jones: Sentinel Lost (excerpt)
Copyright © 2015 by Amy E Jones

Publisher: Gabby Reads Publishing LLC

Cover Designer: http://coveryourdreams.net/
Editor: http://www.demonfordetails.com/

ISBN-10: 1941871062
ISBN-13: 978-1-941871-06-5

Published in the United States of America.

ACKNOWLEDGMENTS

Of course I have people to thank for making this book what it is today. To Gabrielle, my cover artist who gave me a cover with a guy on it this time! And it is a great guy, which was an accomplishment in itself since Jean Luc is, well, *Jean Luc*.

Thanks to Faith who, as usual, made this book even better. Thanks for being as OCD in editing as I am in writing!

To Amy who has been so much more than a formatter to me. Thanks for answering all my questions and teaching me about self-publishing.

Another big thank you to my friend Lara who once again gave me suggestions that made the characters stronger. I may have unleashed a monster in you, but it is productive monster, so I'm very happy.

And to my poet friend Ruth who, like The Fledgling, came up with the title of this work as well. I may have to put you on retainer!

AUTHOR'S NOTE

When I wrote about how Jean Luc and Talia met in The Fledgling, many of you asked why they were no longer together and if their story would have a continuation. Hah! I would never leave you in suspense—for very long that is. I knew when I wrote The Fledgling there would be more coming for them in the future. After all, *we* (you the reader, me the author, and Misha, of course) have known from their first encounter that Jean Luc and Talia are perfect for each other.

Becky –

Thanks for taking this writing journey with me and making it fun in the process. Your support means the world to me.

CHAPTER 1

The woman lying on the lounge chair by the pool was movie-star gorgeous, even in death. Instead of a bathing suit, she wore a barely-there negligee of lavender satin. Early morning sun glinted off her expensively highlighted hair. Long lashes rested against her perfectly formed cheeks. And she had perky, bow lips. Talia had heard the expression but hadn't understood it until today. This woman had obviously lived her life as the center of attention. Had that same attention led to her death?

Well, at least Talia's job with the Bureau of Supernatural Relations was never boring. There was always some supe messing up in front of humans, and she and her partner, Will, would then have to cover it up. But this? Her stomach turned. This wasn't something they could cover up easily.

"Should I call the police?" Will asked.

"No." Talia knelt down and examined the woman more closely.

"No? I don't like where this is going, T. We can't take her body."

Talia stood. "We take bodies all the time."

"Yeah, supe bodies. Never a human."

"Well, there's a first time for everything. If we don't

take her, how are we going to explain to the coroner about the twin puncture wounds on her neck?"

"*Damn.*"

She clenched her fists. *God, what a waste.* "It's still early. Hopefully we don't have too much of a containment issue yet." She looked across the pool to the gangly man pacing back and forth. His T-shirt read *Vegas Pool Services.* "The pool boy found her?"

Will smirked. "The pool *shifter*-boy found her."

Talia cringed inwardly. She should have sensed he was shifter. *Shit.* That meant he'd probably heard what she said. She glanced over at him. Yep, his scowl confirmed it.

What was *wrong* with her? She never slipped up on the job. She was at a murder scene, for God's sake. It had to be the past week catching up with her. Between the shifter rebellion they had just squelched with the help of the Cleveland team and seeing Jean Luc again, she was still out of whack. But Jean Luc was on his way home, and she'd managed to avoid having any type of serious conversation with him.

She took a deep breath. Her personal drama would just have to wait.

"I'll go talk to the witness. Can you pull the van around so we can load her in before the neighborhood wakes up? And give Nicholas a call. We don't need our fearless leader stroking out on us if he hears about this from someone else."

"Sure thing," Will replied.

Talia walked around the pool to the shifter who had stopped pacing and now stood glaring at her.

"Sorry about the pool boy crack; it's been a long morning already."

"Tell me about it. I wasn't expecting to find a dead human at my first stop today."

She held out her hand to him. "I'm Talia Walker from the BSR."

He grabbed her hand and shook it quickly. "Steve Williams."

"How long ago did you find her?"

He checked his watch. "I called your office right away, so about forty-five minutes ago."

"Do you know anything about her?"

"Her name is…was…Melanie Thomas. She was single. She moved in here about a year ago. Told me she was retired."

Talia looked over at the woman lying on the chaise. She couldn't have been much more than thirty. Talia then took in the pool with the high fence surrounding it and the back of the large house before turning back to her witness. Her eyebrows rose in question.

Steve held up his hands. "Hey, I know how it sounds, but that's what she told me. I think she had a sugar daddy or whatever the norms are calling them these days. She paid me on time, and the rest was none of my business."

"Did you ever meet anyone else here?"

"You mean a vamp like you? Nope. I never sensed any supes around here."

Talia narrowed her eyes.

He shrugged. "I saw the bite on her neck when I found her, which is why I called you instead of the cops. This is going to cause big trouble, isn't it?"

Dead human. Killer vampire. She watched Will come around the fence carrying a body bag. Now they were exacerbating the situation by stealing the body. Big trouble? What a monumental understatement.

Jean Luc turned onto the Vegas Strip. At night, humans and supernaturals were drawn to the strip by the neon promise of escape. But as he drove along in the early morning light, the city seemed to wilt in on itself. As did the tourists who trudged from one hotel to the next, determined to see as many glitzy sights as they could.

Jean Luc stopped at the light. He would be facing his own determined female soon enough. In truth, she was not his female anymore. But he planned to rectify the situation. If Talia would let him. She was not expecting him, and he had no idea if the surprise would work to his advantage or make it worse. He was supposed to be on his way back to Cleveland with Kyle and the rest of the team, since the shifter case here was resolved. Instead, he had dropped them at the airport, and Kyle had given him a last minute pep talk.

"Remember, she still cares for you. I can tell."

Jean Luc was not as convinced as Kyle appeared to be, but he was willing to take a chance. He had pulled her duffle bag out of the trunk and placed it in her hands, turning her toward the airport doors. "Text me when you land, *ma petite*."

Kyle spun around. "So what are you going to say to Talia?"

Why did she leave me? Does she still care for me? "I do not know yet."

Kyle scowled at him. "What do you mean, you don't know? Don't you think you should figure those things out first, *before* you go see her? Am I going to have to tell you what to say, too?"

A whistle sounded, and a policeman gestured at him to move along. "I need to move the car, Kyle. Let us discuss this later." He shooed her toward the door.

She had shouted over her shoulder, "Call me when you need help!"

A car horn sounded, and Jean Luc jerked back to the present. The traffic light had turned green. He put his foot on the gas and headed down the strip again.

Talia was still amazing. When he first laid eyes on her again a week ago, her beauty had almost stopped his heart. Not that he needed it to remain beating in order to live. She had cut her hair so it framed her face. It had been gorgeous when it was long and wavy, but now her face was the center of attention. Perfect mocha skin and brown eyes with flecks of gold. When she was angry or aroused, the gold actually glowed. And it was obvious her vampire powers had far surpassed even his expectations when he had trained her thirty years ago.

He still had not prepared anything to say for the moment she opened her door. But something would come to him. He had not remained alive for the past four hundred years without the ability to think on his feet.

His phone beeped, and he glanced over at it on the passenger seat. A text from Kyle flashed on the screen. *Don't blow it, Frenchie.*

CHAPTER 2

Talia closed her eyes and stood perfectly still while the warm water sluiced down her body. Not that a shower could wash away the memory of the dead woman, but she needed a couple minutes to herself.

She was finally alone. The Cleveland supe squad had left early that morning, and five minutes after they left, she and Will had been called out to deal with the body. The past week had been stressful enough—what with shifter pack coups and collateral damage that had turned her house into a temporary hospital.

She turned off the shower and reached for a towel. Oh, who was she kidding? The stress had more to do with one ridiculously confident and sexy vampire.

Jean Luc.

It had been twenty-five years since she'd seen him. How could he still affect her so? He still had that wonderful, long black hair he tied back in a queue. One look into his dark eyes, and the room spun. *Damn him.* But she'd hid her attraction to him well. She'd become a master at burying her emotions. Because he'd not shown *any* emotion. Cool and collected the whole time. And now he was gone. She could return to her normal life. The one she'd chosen when she pushed him away.

But first she needed to track down Melanie's killer.

Talia tucked a towel around her before wandering into her bedroom. She heard a splash and glanced out the window overlooking the back yard. Will was doing his morning laps, his way of relieving stress. It was a cold morning for Vegas, but that didn't keep him from his daily ritual. He hadn't been able to come over during the past week because of all her houseguests, especially since he liked to swim nude. Shifters weren't shy as a rule. She smiled and went to her closet. As far as partners were concerned, he was a good one. If he wanted to swim nude, she didn't have a problem with it. She wasn't shy, either.

After dressing and going downstairs, she decided to make coffee for Will. Even though she couldn't drink it anymore, she still loved the rich fragrance. Maybe she would make him an omelet, too. There was still some food left over. Unless Will brought his own food, her refrigerator was normally bare. Except for her bags of blood, of course.

She padded into the kitchen, started the coffee, then pulled out a frying pan and prepared the eggs. She hadn't cooked anything for herself in decades, but she still remembered how. She used to be a pretty good cook, but eating was one of the pleasures stolen from her, along with her humanity. She tightened her fist around the spatula, bending the metal slightly. *Stop!* She hadn't thought about her turning for a long time, and dwelling on it didn't help. Seeing Jean Luc had brought it all back. If not for him, she might still be in hiding.

Jean Luc was the reason she had finally embraced her vampire nature. It was either that or cease to exist, and she wouldn't give the bastard who turned her the satisfaction. One day, she would find Chris and make him pay.

She watched the eggs bubble in the pan. *Hmm.* Too soon to touch them. Patience was needed when making omelets…and when planning revenge.

After a few moments, she folded the omelet, reached for a plate, and slid the eggs onto it. *Perfect.*

The doorbell rang, and she frowned. Who could that be, at this hour? She headed to the door and faltered as tingling ran up her spine and teased her brain. *Shit.* It couldn't be. There was only one supe who did that to her. She strode to the door and yanked it open.

"Jean Luc."

He didn't answer, instead gazing at her face as if memorizing it.

Her throat tightened. "Has something happened? Where is everyone else?"

"Nothing has happened. I dropped Kyle, Doc, and Jason off at the airport. I am here because there are things I wish to discuss with you."

She took a slow breath to keep her heart from speeding up. She would not let him sense her anxiety. "What do we need to talk about?"

He smiled slightly. "Are you going to invite me in for this discussion?"

Talia shrugged and stepped back from the door, allowing him into the hall but maintaining the distance between them. She led the way into the living room and gestured him to a chair, but he continued standing. The smell of eggs and coffee drifted into the room, and he turned to look toward the kitchen door.

"Have I interrupted something?"

She was not going to take the bait. The sooner he said what he needed to say, the sooner she could usher him out of the house. "What do you need to discuss?"

He hesitated again, which surprised her. Jean Luc was one of the most decisive males she had ever known, supernatural or not.

"I want to know how you are doing."

She resisted the urge to huff like a spoiled schoolgirl. "Jean Luc, what is this? You stayed in my house for a week. And now you came all the way back to ask how I'm doing?"

His eyes tightened. "There was too much pandemonium before, too much that needed to be taken care of. I wanted to speak with you alone. I—"

"Is there a problem?"

Will stood in the doorway, a towel wrapped around his still-damp body. Said towel left nothing to the imagination.

Jean Luc took in Will's appearance, and his eyebrow rose slightly. "There is no problem, is there, Talia?"

"No, everything's fine, Will. Go eat your breakfast."

Will smirked. "You treat me so good, *partner*." He turned and sauntered out of the room.

Talia barely resisted rolling her eyes at his retreating form. *What the hell was that all about?* She turned back to Jean Luc who, if she wasn't mistaken, was gritting his teeth. But that couldn't be right. He couldn't be jealous. Not after she'd left him. Not after all this time.

"What were you saying?"

Jean Luc's gaze moved from the empty doorway to Talia's face. "I want to know that you are doing well, that you are content. Are you happy here in Vegas?"

"Yes. I've settled in. The supernaturals in the city keep us busy, and Will's a good partner. Are *you* happy?"

Jean Luc nodded stiffly. "Yes. Misha and I have been in Cleveland for ten years now."

Talia smiled despite the tension rolling up her spine. "I miss that crazy Russian. Is he still eating enough food for a family of four?"

"Yes. He has turned Kyle into his pastry supplier."

Talia's stomach burned. Kyle. What the hell was she to Jean Luc? She definitely had something going on with the shifter leader, but she bore Jean Luc's mark. He had *bitten* her. Talia bit her lip to keep herself from demanding answers.

Jean Luc continued, "It has been good to stay in one place. Doc and Jason are also wonderful additions to the team."

She nodded. "You have a family now." Which is what Jean Luc needed. And she was still alone. But that had been her choice.

He stared at her hard for a moment and opened his mouth. Were they finally going to get to the reason he came back?

His phone rang, and he closed his eyes at the interruption.

"Are you going to answer it?"

"No."

After a few more rings, the phone went silent. And he took a step closer to her.

Her phone rang. She glanced over at the coffee table where she had left it and saw Nicholas's name flash on the screen.

"Sorry, but I have to get this."

She walked over to the table to pick up the phone. "Nicholas."

"Is Jean Luc with you?"

She turned to face him. "Yes."

"Good. He'll be staying to help with the situation."

She narrowed her eyes at Jean Luc. "We don't need any help."

"I disagree. Bring him up to speed, and when Marty is done with the autopsy, have him call me with the results."

She ended the call.

"What situation?" Jean Luc asked.

Oh no, he wasn't doing this. "Save it. You could have just told me up front that Nicholas had you stay." Of course he hadn't really stayed to see her.

He frowned. "That is not what happened —"

"Sorry to interrupt again," Will announced from the doorway.

Talia swallowed a rude retort. Her partner had horrible timing. But at least this time he was wearing clothes. "What is it?" she snapped.

"Marty just called. He's finished the autopsy."

"Okay, let's get moving, then."

"I am going with you," Jean Luc announced.

Talia glared at him. She didn't have time for an argument, and Jean Luc had four hundred years of stubbornness going for him. "Fine. But I'm the lead on this. Got it?"

His right eyebrow rose infinitesimally. "*Oui.*"

She didn't believe him for a second, especially when he hauled out the French.

CHAPTER 3

Jean Luc prided himself on his self-control. But at this very moment, it took every fiber of his being not to eviscerate the cocky shifter in the passenger seat of the van enjoying the omelet Talia had obviously prepared for him.

What exactly was happening between them? While Jean Luc and the others had been staying at Talia's house, Will had spent little time there. But now he was back. And more than comfortable parading naked in front of Talia. Jean Luc took a deep breath, willing his fangs to retract.

Talia turned off the strip with a screech of tires.

"Damn, T," Will sputtered. "Slow down. I almost lost my breakfast."

"Haven't you finished yet?"

"Hold on a sec," Will said with his mouth full. After a few more moments, he snapped the plastic container shut.

"Who is the victim?" Jean Luc asked.

"Human by the name of Melanie Thomas," Will replied.

"How did she die?"

"Didn't Nicholas already fill you in on all this?" Talia interrupted.

"No. As I have attempted to explain to you, I know nothing about the case."

Talia glared at him in the rearview mirror and then looked back to the road.

"She had fang marks on her neck," Will volunteered.

Mon Dieu. Jean Luc hadn't seen this type of killing in years. It was more like the indiscriminate drainings he and others of similar conviction had fought to eliminate centuries ago.

"Did Marty tell you anything?" Talia asked Will.

"Nope. You know how he is. Likes to have a captive audience when he does his thing." Will looked back at Jean Luc. "Marty is a Traman demon."

Jean Luc nodded. Tramans could be extremely egotistical. "He is a Medical Examiner?"

"He does the ME stuff for us on the side. He's actually an amazing surgeon. But don't tell him I said that." Will grinned. "He worked on both Griffin and Jason's injuries last week."

"I did not have an opportunity to meet him then. I must thank him for his assistance."

Will groaned. "Don't go overboard. He can barely fit his head through the door as it is."

Talia pulled down a side street and parked in front of what appeared to be an abandoned car wash. The three of them climbed out of the van, and Talia unlocked the back door, opening it onto an empty bay with giant scrub brushes mounted on poles. Will pushed back hanging plastic strips, exposing another door. He entered numbers into a keypad, and the door swished open.

Jean Luc followed Will and Talia into a lab much like Doc's lab in Cleveland, complete with an autopsy table and equipment scattered around the room on various tables.

"Yo, Marty!" Will hollered.

A tall male with reddish-blond hair entered the room. "Must you yell, William?"

Will smirked. "Yes, I must, Marty."

Talia rolled her eyes. "Save the pleasantries for later, boys. What have you found out so far?"

Marty shot Jean Luc a pointed look. "First, I believe introductions are in order."

When Talia stood mute, Will chimed in. "Jean Luc Delacroix this is Doctor Martin Stanford *the Third*. But you can just call him Marty."

Marty frowned at Will for a moment before turning to Jean Luc. "I prefer Martin. You're from the Cleveland team. We didn't get to meet last week."

"I was occupied with the cleanup while you helped Jason and Griffin. Thank you."

"Luckily neither of them was hurt badly. Both surgeries were quite routine."

Will coughed and then mumbled something that sounded like "conceited."

Talia interrupted. "What can you tell us about Melanie Thomas?"

Marty picked up a tablet from the table. He touched the screen a couple times and then came back over to the group. "She was killed by a vampire."

Will laughed. "Shit, Marty, I could have told you that."

Marty ignored him and continued. "It isn't that simple. This isn't a case of a vampire accidentally taking too much. She was almost completely drained of blood. They knew exactly what they were doing."

"They?" Jean Luc asked.

"Two different vampires drained her. In addition to the bite on her neck, she also had a bite on her inner thigh."

"Was she raped?" Talia asked, her voice tight.

"There was no evidence of it."

"And you're sure it was two vampires?" Will pushed.

"Yes, the bite wounds are different. They definitely came from two different vamps, but I don't know if they both meant to kill her."

Jean Luc frowned. "Explain, please."

"The bite wound on her thigh was done first. It had already begun to heal."

Talia nodded. "The vampire sealed it after he was done."

"Right. The bite on her neck was still fresh, and since she died, the wounds wouldn't have had time to heal."

"So we don't know if the vamps were working together or not?"

"No. But I did discover something interesting. There was oil on her."

"It's Vegas," Will interjected. "If you don't wear some kind of lotion, you won't last long in the sun."

"I don't mean suntan lotion. You can't buy this oil at the corner store. It is cedar oil, which is actually made from juniper, and has been in use for thousands of years. It was first used as preparation for embalming by the Egyptians."

The hair on the back of Jean Luc's neck stood on end. "Are there any founding vampires living here?"

Talia shook her head. "No. Most of the vampires in Vegas are relatively young. The oldest one we have registered here is two hundred and ten."

"But the supernatural visitors check in with you, correct?" Jean Luc asked.

"They should, yes," Talia replied. "Is there something you'd like to share with us?"

How much should he say?

She stared at him pointedly. "Jean Luc?"

He let out the breath he had been holding. "Centuries ago, vampires used ancient oils as a part of rituals."

"What types of rituals?"

"Christening a new founding vampire…and turnings."

Talia's eyes flared, and she visibly tensed. "Do you think this was an attempted turning?"

"I did not say that. But whoever did this used the oil for a very specific reason. We just need to learn the reason."

Talia took a deep breath, appearing to collect herself. "Will, would you call the office and have Susannah find out if any older vamps have reported in lately?"

He pulled his phone out of his pocket. "I'll go call her now."

She turned to Marty. "Did you find a large amount of oil on her, like they had purposely rubbed it on her, or just a little bit, like it had come off one of the vamps?"

"It wasn't residual. They had rubbed it all over her."

Talia blew out a breath. "So where did Melanie meet two vampires?"

"I found other scars on her. She's been bitten before."

"Maybe her sugar daddy has fangs?"

Jean Luc frowned. "I am not following you, Talia."

"A sugar daddy is a rich man who pays for a woman's home and amenities…clothing, furnishings, basically everything she needs to live."

He held up his hand. "I know what the term means. Why do you think she had one?"

"Melanie Thomas was in her early thirties, single, and lived in a huge house. She told our witness she was *retired*. Unless she has family money, I don't know how she could have lived that way without financial support. Did we get a background check back on her yet?"

Marty nodded and tapped on his tablet again. "Susannah sent it over. According to this, she didn't come from money. Both her parents are deceased, and she was an only child."

Will walked back into the room. "A group of vamps has been staying at the Cosmo for a few days now." He turned to Jean Luc. "The Cosmopolitan is a new hotel catering to vamps. But Susannah said none of the group is more than five hundred years old. She texted me their names."

"How many vampires?" Jean Luc asked.

Will checked his phone. "Ten."

Jean Luc frowned. "Which probably means it is a contingent for a founding vampire."

"How do you know?" Will asked.

"Unlike shifters, who are pack-oriented, vampires do not normally travel in large groups. More than likely, a founding vampire is staying there as well. They also do not normally announce their presence. If they have any enemies—and most do—they are not very forthcoming regarding their whereabouts."

Will shook his head. "Wow, you guys are too complex. Glad T isn't mixed up in all this crap."

Talia grimaced. "I'm a vampire, which means I'm mixed up in it whether I want to be or not. I think we need to pay a visit to the Cosmo."

Jean Luc shook his head. "We know nothing about these vampires. And more than likely, none of them would be up this early. Will, would you text me the names as well so I can share them with Misha? He should be able to ferret out more information about them. Once we know who they are, we can decide how to approach them."

"I had forgotten how cautious you can be," Talia replied.

"And I had forgotten how impetuous you can be. You remind me of Kyle."

Talia's eyes flashed gold before she quickly tamped down whatever emotion had caused them to flare. He opened his mouth to ask what was wrong, but Will interrupted him.

"Got to love Kyle. She's something, all right."

Jean Luc stared at Talia. "Yes, she is, but her *enthusiasm* can lead to trouble."

"Fine. We'll wait to hear back from Misha. But not too long. These killers need to be stopped."

"It should only take him a couple hours to gather the pertinent information. In the meantime, we should learn all we can about Melanie Thomas."

"We can't interrogate anyone about her," Talia argued. "No one knows she's dead."

"True. But as Misha has taught me, computers can provide what we need if we know where to look. Credit cards are a fount of information."

Will rubbed his hands together. "Follow the money. I can help with that."

Marty said, "I'm on duty at the hospital. Call if you need anything. Will can use the computer in my office. But don't move anything around on my desk."

"Yes, *sir*."

Marty and Will left, and Jean Luc turned back to Talia.

They were finally alone.

CHAPTER 4

Talia stood in the center of the room, rooted to the spot. Why had she not thought of tracking Melanie's finances? She was acting like a novice. She'd been working on the supe squad for thirty years and had been a bounty hunter before that. She knew better. Why did Jean Luc rattle her so?

"While we wait for Misha's info, why don't I drive you back to your car so you can check into a hotel?" she asked.

He frowned. "We need to talk, Talia."

"Will and I can handle the case. Nicholas didn't have to order you to stay."

"Nicholas is not the reason I am here."

"If he didn't tell you to stay, then why did you come back?"

"Because I have to know. Why did you leave me, Talia?"

Her breathing sped up at his words. "I told you back then. I had to make it on my own."

His eyes locked on her. "And you have done quite well on your own for twenty-five years. You have proven yourself."

If he only knew how much his praise meant to her. "Thank you."

He cleared his throat. "But I hope proving your independence does not mean that you plan to remain alone for the rest of your life."

God, she had no comeback for that. She didn't want to be alone anymore. He was right. She had felt the need to prove herself. To be sure she could stand on her own two feet and not have to rely on anyone. But maybe now she *was* ready to rely on someone. Would Jean Luc be willing to try again?

But it wasn't that simple. She had never told him the truth about her turning. That she had known her sire before he turned her, had been involved with him. She hadn't dared tell him when they first met, and now the lie had morphed into a chasm. But maybe a chasm was too dramatic a word. Could she repair this by simply telling him the truth?

The thought rocked her back on her heels. Being with him again...was it what she truly wanted?

"Talia. Did you hear what I said? I do not want you to be alone...You could come back to Cleveland and join the team."

She gazed into his face. As usual, his emotions were well hidden. But for a second she saw a flash of something in his eyes—pity?—and her stomach dropped.

Had she been reading too much into his words? He was talking about her joining the team not asking her to be with him again. Did he pity her? She could handle many things from Jean Luc, but not pity.

"I'm not alone," she blurted.

His eyes flared red. "Of course. It was presumptuous of me to assume you are not involved with someone."

Oh, shit. She closed her eyes. That's not what she'd meant. Now what? Before she could decide what to say, Jean Luc spoke again.

"Take me back to my car, Talia. I will see about finding a room. Once we have solved the case, I will return to Cleveland."

She nodded. A flood of emotions caused a drought of words. She would tell him the truth about her past as soon as she figured out what to say.

Jean Luc stood in the middle of his hotel room clenching his fists and taking deep, measured breaths. He had made an absolute mess of things. Of course, she had moved on to someone else. Unlike him, she would not cling to a relationship that had ended more than two decades ago. She was young. Twenty-five years was still a long time for her. For some time before he had met her, twenty-five years had not seemed very long. Now? In some ways it was an eternity.

He had tried. Kyle had not been correct in her belief that Talia still wanted him, but he had needed to find out whether there might be a chance for them. Now what he needed was to solve this case so he could get as far away from Talia Walker as possible, as soon as possible.

His phone rang. He glanced at the screen and answered it. "What have you found out, Misha?"

"And a good day to you, too, my friend. You have gotten thrown into another case already, I see."

"Yes. Have you collected the background information?"

"I'm forwarding it to you now. You can open it on your phone, but it would be easier to do it on a computer."

"I will go back to the lab and review the data."

"How is Talia doing?"

"She is fine."

"Fine? Have you been able to spend some time with her?"

"Of course. We are working the case together."

Misha swore in Russian. "Jean Luc —"

"Tell me about the vampires, Misha. We need to figure out who the killers are."

"This group is from Europe. From Spain and Portugal, to be specific."

Jean Luc interrupted. "I am aware of three founding vampires in that region."

"Yes." The sounds of a clicking keyboard came through the phone. "Diego Castillo, Claudio Chavez, and Renato Henriques."

The third name sucked the air from Jean Luc's lungs. He had hoped never to hear it again. An unrealistic expectation, he knew, but most of the older European vampires avoided the US. "So more than likely one of these three are here. But the question is why?"

"Maybe he just wanted to check out Vegas?"

It was never that simple. "Can you find out if there have been reports in Europe of humans being drained?"

"I'm already on it. I've linked into *La Société's* database."

"*La Société* doesn't normally like to work with us. Did they give you any trouble?"

Misha chuckled. "What our European counterparts don't know won't hurt them."

"Be careful, Misha. We do not need them contacting Nicholas."

"No worries, my friend. Now tell me what you're going to do about Talia."

"I have to go. I must update Talia about this information. Keep me apprised of what else you find out."

Misha growled, "Fine for now. But we *will* talk about her later."

Jean Luc drove to the lab and parked his rental car in an empty lot. Had Talia and Will gone to the Cosmopolitan without him? He sat silent for a moment and concentrated. Light tingling ran up his spine. Talia was still inside. He walked through the building to the lab entrance and punched in the numbers he had watched Will input earlier. The door swished open. Two steps into the empty room, and a voice called to him.

"I'm in the back. Come down the hall."

So she still sensed him keenly as well. He grinned at her unnecessary directions. He would have found her regardless. She sat at a computer behind a large desk piled high with folders and papers covering every inch.

"*This* is Marty's office?"

She chuckled. "Yes. Believe it or not. He's a brilliant doctor, but his filing skills leave much to be desired."

"And he was worried about Will moving something? How would he know if he did?"

"Oh, he would know, trust me."

"Where is Will?"

"He went down the street to a drive-through to grab lunch. He has a big appetite. Not as big as Misha's, but his shifter metabolism pretty much means he can eat anything."

"I have heard from Misha. He sent us a file of information regarding the vampires."

She pushed back from the desk. "Have a seat so you can bring it up."

He opened up the computer file. Talia stood behind him to review the screen. As he read the names and notes that Misha had made, she leaned over his shoulder. He inhaled her lavender fragrance. *Mon Dieu*, he had missed that scent. He could not keep himself from looking up into her face. After a few seconds, she turned to him, her eyes widening when she noticed their close proximity.

Before he could say anything, she took a quick step back just as Will bustled into the room, and crumpled a takeout bag in his hands. He lobbed the bag over his head like a basketball. It landed in the garbage can across the room.

"Three points!" He grinned at Talia. "Did I miss anything?"

Talia shook her head. "We were just looking at the vampire data Misha sent us. They're from Europe." She turned back to Jean Luc. "Do you know any of them?"

He stared at her for a moment before responding. "Not personally, no. But I recognize a couple names. They have played some minor roles in the vampire council over the centuries."

Will walked over, and Jean Luc stood to allow him to review the list.

"So do you still think they're a contingent for a founding vampire?" Will asked.

"Most definitely."

Talia jumped in. "Do you have an idea who the founding vampire is?"

"There are three possibilities. We will have to wait

to find out. What about you, Will? Have you learned anything about Melanie Thomas?"

Will nodded and started entering information on the computer. "She wasn't afraid to spend money. Had accounts at several of the high-end shops in town. I have a friend who is checking on her credit cards. Let's see if he's found anything yet." He clicked a few more times. "Got an email from him." Will read the message and smiled. "Apparently, Melanie liked to frequent The Cosmopolitan."

Could it really be that easy? Jean Luc doubted it, but at least now they were armed with solid information. "Are you ready to question our suspects?"

Talia's eyes flashed gold. He took that as a yes.

CHAPTER 5

Talia stepped into the hotel lobby. Cool air enveloped her as the sliding doors automatically closed behind them. In comparison to the Vegas afternoon sun, the lighting inside was muted to accommodate vampire eyes. The lobby decor was reminiscent of a Fred Astaire and Ginger Rogers movie. Everything was black and white with shades of gray, except for little pops of red interspersed throughout the lobby. If Misha saw this, he would gush over it and then plan a vintage movie marathon.

Jean Luc's phone beeped, and he looked at the screen and scowled.

"Ready?" she asked.

He nodded and put the phone back into his pocket.

Talia took the lead, and Jean Luc and Will trailed behind her to the concierge desk. A vampire wearing a very expensive black suit with a blood red, silk handkerchief in his lapel pocket stood behind the desk. His gaze moved over the three of them while they approached, quickly gauging what they were.

"How may I help you?" he asked Jean Luc.

Talia wasn't surprised the concierge turned to him first. Will would be the lowest on this vamp's list since he was a shifter. Jean Luc was the most powerful and oldest vampire, so he would defer to him. But it still rankled a bit.

"We are from the BSR. We need to speak with your manager," Jean Luc replied after glancing at her.

The concierge nodded and pressed a button on his desk. Talia turned toward the reservation desk, expecting to see Roland, the daytime manager she'd dealt with on a previous occasion. The door behind the desk opened to reveal a female vampire who was definitely *not* the day manager. She wore a black suit, if a skin-tight skirt and jacket could be considered a suit. She moved like a dancer, and her blond hair was piled on top of her head like a Forties pinup model. Ruby red lipstick highlighted her lips.

Talia glanced at Will, who was ogling the vamp unashamedly. Talia didn't dare look at Jean Luc's expression.

The manager glided to a stop in front of them, her eyes locking on Jean Luc. "I am Veronique. How may I assist you?"

And of course she was French, because that was how Talia's life worked.

"Jean Luc Delacroix. This is Talia Walker and Will Seaver. We are from the BSR. We need to speak with you in private."

"*Oui.* Of course. Follow me, *s'il vous plaît.*"

Was it Talia's imagination, or did the manager's eyes take on a predatory gleam when she realized Jean Luc was French?

Veronique lead them to a small conference room and closed the door once they were all inside. Jean Luc's phone beeped again. This time he didn't even take it out of his pocket.

"Is there a problem?" she asked, her complete, undivided attention remaining on Jean Luc.

Talia glanced over at Will, who smirked at her.

"We would like to ask you about one of your customers — Melanie Thomas."

Veronique frowned then bit her bottom lip. "Melanie is an...acquaintance of one of our guests."

Talia spoke up. "Is this guest here now?"

"*Oui.*"

"What is his name?"

"Simon Jamison."

Will typed the name into his cell phone, pulled up Simon's picture from the BSR database, and showed it to both Talia and Jean Luc.

"We need to speak with him," Talia pushed.

Veronique hesitated. "He is hosting an event for recent guests who have arrived from Europe. This particular group has requested privacy while they are here and have compensated the hotel for this service."

"The BSR takes precedence over any arrangements you may have made with the group. We, of course, will be as discreet as possible, but we must speak with them," Jean Luc replied.

Veronique pouted for a moment and Talia was barely able to resist laughing. It was like watching a slutty French cartoon.

"You will take us to them," Jean Luc stated in his quiet, powerful way.

Veronique bent her head forward slightly as a sign of submission and sauntered toward the door. Was is Talia's imagination, or was there less sway to her hips?

On the way up the elevator, Jean Luc's phone beeped again.

Will smiled. "You're getting more texts than a thirteen-year-old girl."

Jean Luc didn't respond; he simply turned his phone to silent and stuffed it back into his pocket.

The elevator doors opened to a floor obviously designed for more elite guests. The carpeting and wallpaper had a level of opulence missing from the lobby.

"They are in the room across the hall," Veronique announced.

As soon as Talia, Jean Luc, and Will exited, Veronique pushed the elevator button and the doors shut, leaving them alone in the hall.

Will opened the door, and Talia stepped into a low-lit room and stared in disbelief. A dozen or so vampire males were scattered around the room. And draped on many of them were human females. Working in Vegas, Talia was faced with legalized prostitution every day. She didn't have to like it, but she had to accept it. But this? This was different. The women were all dressed to kill and beautiful, but desperation clung to them like a second skin. Talia had seen that look before on the streets. It was the look of an addict.

"Damn," Will muttered, beside her.

Talia turned to Jean Luc, who crossed his arms as he studied the room.

A few moments later, one of the vampires hurried toward them. He was dressed in a business suit and matched the picture Will had showed them.

"I'm sorry, but this is a closed event," he said.

"Simon Jamison?"

He frowned. "Yes."

"I'm Talia Walker from the BSR. We need to talk to you."

"This is an inappropriate time."

Talia smiled even though she wanted to smack the smug look off his face. "My intent is to avoid causing a scene, but I will if you don't come with me now."

Simon opened his mouth as if to argue until Jean Luc stepped up next to her.

"Please do not make this any more difficult than it needs to be."

Simon huffed and walked down the hall and into an empty conference room. Talia, Jean Luc, and Will followed.

"What is so important that could not wait until later?" Simon asked.

"We understand that you're acquainted with Melanie Thomas," Talia responded.

He narrowed his eyes. "What about her?"

"Please explain your relationship."

"Did she steal something again from one of the stores? I don't know why she keeps doing that. I give her plenty of money."

"And why, exactly, do you give her money?" Talia asked.

He looked away for a moment before continuing. "Melanie and I have an arrangement."

"An arrangement that includes sex and blood?"

He still avoided Talia's eyes. "There is nothing illegal about helping a friend financially."

Talia's stomach twisted. "And does your relationship include sharing her with others?"

Simon cleared his throat. "She is willing to be adventurous." He rushed on. "She is a consenting adult."

"She *was* a consenting adult. Melanie is dead."

His eyes widened. "How?"

"She was drained."

He paled. "I did not kill her."

"No one said you did," Jean Luc replied.

He glanced frantically between her and Jean Luc. "I wasn't the only one who spent time with her."

Talia shook her head. "Glad to see you're so broken up about her death."

Simon's fangs lengthened. "I don't need to answer to you, fledgling."

She took a step closer and got right into his face. "Since I work for the BSR, actually, you do."

Simon tensed, but before he could make a move, he froze, his eyes widening slightly. A burst of power surged over her from the right, where Jean Luc was standing. She didn't take her eyes off Simon, but she could imagine what Jean Luc's face looked like. It took a lot to make Jean Luc angry, but once you did, watch out.

Simon backed up a step. "Melanie frequented the hotel regularly. She could have met anyone here."

"Were you with Melanie last night?" Will jumped in.

"Yes."

"Did you bite her?" Jean Luc asked.

Simon hesitated.

Talia shrugged, although she was feeling anything but nonchalant. "If you don't tell us, we could make you give us a bite impression. Our Medical Examiner will analyze it."

"Yes. I bit her."

"Where?"

His eyes narrowed. "Where? She had more than one bite mark? I bit her on the thigh. That is the only place I ever bit her. She was too perfect to mar where people could see."

Talia shook her head. "She wasn't a doll. She was a person, and now she's dead."

"Well, I didn't kill her. I'm innocent!"

"Innocent? She gritted her teeth to stop her fangs from extending. "You're a blood pimp."

His mouth fell open, and he sputtered. "I am not a pimp."

"You gave Melanie money for her blood and sex, plus you shared her with others? What the hell else would you call it?"

"She got a lot out of the relationship. She was not some poor, picked-upon human."

"No, she was an addict. You got her addicted to the pull, didn't you? And what about the women in the other room? Do you support them financially as well?"

He straightened. "Those other women are not your business. Find out who killed Melanie. Are we done here?"

"For now. Do not leave Las Vegas," Jean Luc demanded.

Will snarled at Simon as he walked past. "What a slimeball."

Talia grimaced. "Let's talk to some of the other women."

"Simon isn't going to be happy," Will grinned.

"Tough."

Thirty minutes later, Talia had learned two things. These women were leading desperate, blood-addicted lives, and none of them had liked Melanie Thomas. Apparently, Melanie hadn't been friendly at all with the other women. She was a backstabber according to one, and that was the nicest word any of them had used to describe her.

What had turned Melanie into a backstabbing bitch? Was it the addiction? Or was it something more fundamental? Talia shook her head. She'd had enough. She nodded tightly to Will and left the room. It was time for a little heart-to-heart with Veronique.

Talia found her quarry in the lobby. She was standing next to the concierge desk with her hand on her hip, laughing at something the concierge said.

"Yo, Veronica."

She jerked at Talia's voice and spun toward her, eyes narrowing. "My name is Veronique."

"Do you have any idea what is going on in your swanky hotel?"

"I don't know what you mean."

But the female looked to the left when she answered. Which was a tell. And in Vegas, you quickly learned to look for tells. Veronique was lying. She knew exactly what was going on.

"If I learn you are continuing to have these types of private events here, I will shut down the hotel. *Comprenez-vous?*"

Veronique's mouth fell open in shock, but only for a moment. Her face reddened, and then she responded in rapid-fire French. If Talia wasn't mistaken, she was cursing. Jean Luc and Will both walked up then, and Veronique turned to Jean Luc and continued ranting in French. Jean Luc responded in French as well.

Talia turned away, leaving Jean Luc to deal with the French version of Jessica Rabbit. Will whistled softly as he followed her.

"I think you might have just channeled Kyle. Holy crap, T. You are downright sexy when you get all riled up like that."

"Cut it out, Will." She gripped her hands together to keep them from shaking.

Will grabbed her hands and turned her to face him. His usual grin was replaced by a set mouth and eyes narrowed in concern. "Talia, take a deep breath and let it out slowly."

She didn't argue. He took deep breaths along with her while she stared into his green eyes.

Her heart had finally started to calm down until she

saw Jean Luc standing across the lobby watching the two of them. He looked down at their joined hands, and his eyes flashed red for a second. But just as quickly, his face lost all expression, to be replaced by a stone mask.

CHAPTER 6

Jean Luc had to escape his hotel room, even if it meant being surrounded by Vegas tourists. He couldn't sleep. Misha had been texting him nonstop. Leave it to his demon partner to frustrate him through technology.

Plus, his mind kept replaying the scene with Will and Talia endlessly. He had sensed Talia's anxiety across the lobby and had simply turned away from Veronique, who still had been sputtering her displeasure. But before he could reach Talia, Will comforted her. Will touched her. Not him.

Jean Luc walked along the strip, weaving through the crowd. He could sense various supernaturals as he traveled by a faint buzzing along his spinal column. After a few minutes, the buzzing became more pronounced and focused. He was being followed.

So much for clearing his head.

He headed down a side street away from the people and turned into a small alley.

"Jean Luc. Wait!"

He stopped and spun at the sound of the familiar voice. *It could not be.*

"Damn. It *is* you. I don't believe it!"

"Leo?"

"Yes." He stepped further into the alley, and the

light from a pole illuminated the vampire who had saved Jean Luc's life countless times.

The deep voice caused memories to rise up and swamp him. A time of blood and battles and not knowing if they would live to see another day. Even though Leo's long hair and beard were now replaced by a buzz cut and bare face, Jean Luc would have recognized his friend anywhere.

Leo stepped forward, pulled Jean Luc into his arms, and crushed him against a hard chest, then held him back and gazed at him. "God, it has been too long, my friend."

Jean Luc nodded, his throat closing as words failed him. "How...why..."

"It is a bit of a story. Instead of telling it in an alley, let's find a more comfortable spot to converse."

Ten minutes later, they sat in an empty bar at a corner table, pretending to nurse beers.

"Why are you here, Leo? I thought you were still in Europe."

"I followed a group of vampires. There has been some issues in the past few months, and I was sent to make sure nothing happened here."

Jean Luc's eyebrow shot up. "You work for *La Société*?"

"*Sí.*"

"Why have I not heard your name in connection with them before?"

Leo hesitated. "I'm not your standard employee."

Was he one of the elite vampires who worked in secret? "You are an enforcer now?"

He flashed a grin. "I didn't say that, now did I?"

Jean Luc frowned.

"Hey, why the long face? It's a job that isn't boring, and I get to travel."

"What sort of trouble are you investigating?"

"There have been some attacks on humans."

Jean Luc let out a hard breath. "Well, now we have a dead human here in Vegas. The contingent of vampires staying at The Cosmopolitan work for Renato, correct?"

"Yes. So you haven't seen him yet."

"No, he was not in attendance at the event we visited tonight. And you are following him? We should have killed him when we had the chance centuries ago."

"He is not all bad, Jean Luc. He was thrust into The Wars, just as we were. He did not turn us."

"He was one of LeBlanc's lieutenants. Standing by and doing nothing is not much better. He was not blameless back then. How do you know he is not the one killing humans?"

"More than likely, it is one of his contingent." He tapped his fingers on the table. "We have all changed since those dark days."

Jean Luc nodded grimly and thought back to the vampires with human women draped all over them. Maybe they had not changed enough.

"I have not forgotten, Leo."

Leo's eyes narrowed on him, and he shook his head. "Jean Luc —"

"I owe you my life."

"You are so noble, dear friend. I told you at the time that you didn't need to swear a blood oath to me."

"I will not forget about it. And I will not rescind it."

Leo inclined his head slightly. "I hope to never have use for it." He leaned back in the booth. "Do you like working for the BSR?"

Jean Luc was grateful for the change of subject. "*Oui.*"

Leo ran his fingers along the glass rim in front of him. "I saw you leave the hotel with a female. She is on your team?"

"She is a member of the BSR."

"Is she yours?"

Jean Luc frowned. "No one owns her."

Leo held up his hands. "I meant no offense. From what I could see, she was quite striking."

"Yes."

Leo stared hard at him. "She may not be yours, but you want her all the same."

"It does not matter what I want. She is taken."

"Is she mated?"

"No."

"Then all is not lost."

Jean Luc wanted to argue, but he let it go. Leo would not understand. *Mon Dieu*, truth be told, he did not understand himself.

Jean Luc sat on his hotel balcony, watching the sun rise. After leaving Leo, he had not bothered to go to bed. There was no point to it. His memories were not going to grant him respite. It had been almost four hundred years, but he still vividly remembered that first time waking as a vampire. Sitting up and looking around the field of bodies. Friends and family. *Mon Dieu*, Jacqueline! And the smell of their blood drenching the ground had called to him. But he fought against the beast that had been unleashed in him that day. He would not commit sacrilege and touch their blood.

He had run from the field and retched unceasingly.

He had refused to feed for weeks, until he was so weak he could not hold his head up. He did not deserve to live, not when everyone else was dead, gone. *Why had they left him alone? Why was he chosen to survive?*

In the end, it had been Leo who saved him.

Jean Luc closed his eyes for a second before opening them again to stare at the strip and the people ambling back to their hotel rooms after a night of gambling. Another new day. He stood and walked back into his room. Talia and Will would be picking him up shortly, so he took a quick shower and dressed.

When he felt the familiar sensation at the back of his neck, he ground his teeth. It was not possible. He yanked open the hotel door.

Misha stood in the hall. "Hello, my friend."

Jean Luc turned and stalked back into the hotel room. "Why are you here?"

"You didn't answer my texts."

"No, I did not."

"Why?"

"*Mon Dieu!* Because you were texting me every five minutes!"

"Because you weren't answering me. So I had to come, since I thought you might need my help."

"Nicholas sent you?"

"No. I borrowed Boris's plane."

"Your father allowed you to bring the jet back here after it just returned to Cleveland?"

"He was hesitant at first, but once I explained what you were doing, he agreed that you would screw things up without my help."

"I can handle a case on my own."

Misha smiled innocently. "It's not the case I'm worried about."

Jean Luc glowered at him, which only made Misha's smile broaden.

"I am not scared of you, vampire. You forget I have lived with your prickly disposition for a long time."

Jean Luc refused to respond, changing the subject instead. "Who did you leave in charge at home? Kyle?"

"No. Kyle is spending time with Griffin."

"They have made up?" Jean Luc blurted, shocked.

"Kyle refused to let him push her away. Said she was going to knock some sense into him if she had to."

Jean Luc grinned. "Good for her."

"I never thought I would say this, but you could learn from Kyle. You and Talia are meant to be together."

He would not take the bait. "Then who did you leave in charge?"

Misha sighed. "I called Jasper and Colin. It's pretty uneventful for them in Columbus now that college football season is over. So they drove up to cover for us. I take it from your change of subject that you haven't talked to Talia yet?"

Jean Luc managed not to growl. "I spoke with Talia. She is not interested in renewing our relationship."

"She said that?"

"*Oui.*"

Misha studied him like a specimen under a microscope. "She said she did not want to be with you anymore."

"She is involved with someone else. She will not tell me who, but I think it is her partner, Will."

"Is she in love with him?"

Jean Luc's stomach twisted. "I did not ask her that. What does it matter?"

Misha's head tilted back, and he looked at the ceiling. "You stupid vampire. It means everything." He tipped his head forward and glared at Jean Luc. "It's a good thing I'm here."

A knock at the door interrupted Jean Luc's response. He opened the door to Talia and Will. Talia's eyes widened, and she smiled. A brilliant smile that caused Jean Luc's heart to stutter.

"Misha!"

She rushed around him, flung herself into Misha's outstretched arms, and laughed while he swung her around in a circle.

Jean Luc's chest burned. He would give anything for her to smile at him that way.

CHAPTER 7

Misha enveloped Talia in a bear hug. Tears stung her eyes, and she concentrated on not letting them escape. After he was done spinning her around, she clung to him a bit longer than necessary. He stepped back and held her at arm's length.

"I did not think it possible that you could be more gorgeous than you were the last time I saw you, but it's true. I would say you have the face of an angel, but I've met some and they are not as beautiful as you."

Her face heated and she shrugged out of his grip. "Cut it out, you crazy Russian. The last thing we need right now are pissed-off angels knocking on our door. This is my partner, Will."

Will held his hands out in front of him, palms out. "No offense, big guy, but there will be no hugging."

Misha chuckled. "No worries."

Talia looked between Misha and Jean Luc. "Why are you here?"

Misha shrugged. "I missed all the excitement last week, so when Jean Luc contacted me about the new case, I decided to come."

She put her hands on her hips, but she couldn't keep the humor out of her voice. "You don't think I can handle my own case?"

"Of course! The case was just an excuse to come see you. Kyle told me you have a nice house, and I can't wait to spend time with you again. I was confused when I found out Jean Luc is staying in this hotel and not with you."

"Well..." Talia struggled for her next words.

"He stayed at your house last week, did he not?"

"Yes."

"And we are working on an important case, so it makes sense for us to be close by in the event something happens, yes?"

"Right."

Misha grinned. "It's settled, then. We'll stay with you. It will be like old times. Now, let me fill you in on what I've learned about the contingent of vampires over breakfast. I'm famished."

Talia laughed. "You never change."

Misha's ice blue eyes twinkled. "But you love me just the same."

———————

Talia smirked at Will's wide-eyed expression. Misha had just finished another pancake. She'd lost count of how many he had eaten. Even the waitress was suitably impressed. She walked over again and smiled at Misha.

"Would you like some more pancakes?"

Misha wiped his mouth with his napkin and shook his head. "No, that will be it for me, Monica. But they were delicious. Will?"

Will chuckled. "I was full three servings ago, but I would like some more coffee."

"Coming right up." Monica hustled away with the

empty plates and then topped off Will's mug. She held it up to both Jean Luc and Talia, who shook their heads. They had both ordered coffee so as not to look too strange. Of course, thanks to Misha's eating extravaganza, they were not the ones who stood out.

Misha winked at Monica, and she blushed and rushed away.

Talia shook her head. "Can we get down to business, now that your stomach has been taken care of?"

"Of course. Jean Luc's instinct was correct. My research on our European—" Misha glanced around the room "—*guests* is that they do work for one of the founding v's."

"Renato Henriques," Jean Luc announced.

"Yes." Misha's chest deflated a bit. "How did you know?"

"I ran into an old acquaintance."

"Someone with the contingent?" Talia asked.

"No, he works for *La Société*. He is following the contingent. Apparently, there have been some incidents in Europe recently. Some attacks."

Talia sat up straighter. "So we're on to something with this group. Melanie probably met the killer at the hotel."

"It could be Renato himself," Jean Luc replied.

"Have you met this Renato before?"

Jean Luc hesitated for a moment before responding. "We met a long time ago."

"And what does your friend say?" Talia asked.

"That it is more than likely someone else in the contingent."

"And who is this friend?" Misha asked.

"Leonardo Salazar."

Misha frowned. "That name is not on *La Société's* employee list."

"Now you're pulling my leg," Will jumped in. "You know the list by heart?"

"I recently reviewed the names, and since I have a photographic memory, they stuck."

"He is a new member."

Talia stared at Jean Luc for a second. She didn't know why, but Jean Luc had just lied to Misha.

Misha continued. "So *La Société* is jumping into the mix. This case is getting more complicated by the second, my friend."

Jean Luc's mouth tightened. "I think we are missing something important. Why is Renato here in the first place? There must be a reason why he left Europe to come here."

"So let's go talk to him and find out," Talia answered.

Talia stood outside closed double doors. Matching vampire security guards stood like bookends on either side. The team had decided that only Jean Luc and Talia should approach Renato. The founding vampire would not want a shifter or a demon anywhere near him. And from the looks of his guards, they would not be happy either. If they were ever happy.

"We need to speak to Renato Henriques," Talia stated.

"There is no one by that name here," the guard on the right replied.

"Then who are you guarding?"

"No one."

"You are standing at attention outside an empty room? Then you won't mind if I check it out."

They stepped in front of her. Vamp Guard One spoke again. "You can't go in there."

"Yes, I can."

Vamp Guard Two growled.

Jean Luc rested his hand on her arm. "Talia, wait. If a founding vampire is indeed in there, the room should be treated like an embassy."

"Maybe. But since I've been told no one is in there, then it doesn't need to be treated that way."

The door opened, and petite brunette said something in what sounded like Spanish but was different. Portuguese, maybe? The two vamps backed to either side of the door again. The female beckoned her and Jean Luc into the room. Before Talia stepped through the door, Jean Luc grabbed her arm.

"Please let me interrogate him."

Warmth surged up her arm from his touch. It was a combination of his power and the sensations he brought to life in her normally dormant body. She nodded, and he let go. Her arm cooled, and her heart crept back into its bunker.

She took a calming breath as they stepped inside the room. The suite was quite ordinary. There was a massage table set up to the side of the couch, and a vampire lay face down with a sheet draped over him.

The female picked up a fresh towel and quickly wiped off the vampire's back and legs before handing him a robe. He stood, letting the sheet fall.

Talia was not impressed.

He pulled on the robe and tied the sash. The female grabbed the sheet from the floor and hurried out of the room. Talia hadn't known what to expect, but Renato looked as ordinary as the room around him. He was average height with short brown hair and dark eyes.

Jean Luc inclined his head slightly. "Renato."

"Jean Luc. It has been a while. I heard you had left Europe over a century ago. I'm surprised you settled here." He turned to Talia. "And who is this?"

"This is Talia Walker. She is a member of the Bureau of Supernatural Relations."

"Ah, yes. The American version of *La Société*." He turned back to Jean Luc, dismissing Talia. "Is there some sort of problem?"

Jean Luc continued. "We are surprised to find you here. Your contingent registered with us upon arrival, but you were not listed."

Renato shrugged his shoulders. "An oversight on my secretary's part. I will discuss it with her. I apologize for any inconvenience it may have caused you."

Jean Luc inclined his head. "Of course."

Renato straightened the right cuff and then the left on his robe. "If we have finished, then? I have a busy schedule."

"Actually, we have additional questions for you," Jean Luc replied.

"In what regard?"

"A woman was killed two nights ago."

He shrugged again. "And why would that be my concern?"

"She was drained."

Renato frowned. "While that is troublesome, I do not know why you would see the need to speak to me about it."

"We understand there have been several attacks against humans in Europe. In areas where you and your contingent have been traveling."

Renato's eyes narrowed. "You have been speaking to someone at *La Société*?"

"We are speaking of murder. Cooperation is needed."

"Let us not make a mountain out of a molehill, as Americans like to say. This is a *human* woman, after all."

Talia tensed, and Jean Luc glanced at her. She bit her lip and let him continue, even though it was killing her.

"When exposure of our kind is at stake, every precaution should be taken."

Renato nodded for Jean Luc to continue.

"Is there anyone in your contingent who has been acting strangely? Someone with the beginning signs of bloodlust?"

"No. I have no problems with my people, Jean Luc. You are following the wrong path. Now I must get ready for my next meeting. If you will excuse me?"

Talia stepped forward. "May I ask you one thing?"

"Go ahead."

"Why are you in Vegas?"

Renato smiled, and Talia's stomach turned at his sleazy expression. "I have always wanted to see Las Vegas. It is the American pinnacle of excess. This country is an example of true decadence. I decided to try a taste."

When they exited the room, Talia felt the urge to run home and shower. She grinned at Vamp One and Vamp Two, who scowled back at her. On their way down the hall toward the elevator, they ran into the female vampire masseuse. Jean Luc smiled at her, and she smiled right back, showing a little fang, *the ho.*

"I will catch up with you in a moment, Talia."

Talia barely kept her mouth from hanging open before nodding. She walked away toward the elevator, where she hit the down button and watched the numbers on the panel creep up ever so slowly. A feminine chuckle sounded behind her, and she bit the inside of her cheek. *Don't look over your shoulder. Don't look...damn it.* She looked. The female was handing Jean Luc a piece of paper.

Talia took a deep breath to stop the steam from coming out of her ears. She had no right to be upset that Jean Luc was chatting up the pretty masseuse in some sexy language that rolled off his tongue as easily as French did. He was a talented vampire. *Focus!* She was *so* not going there.

The elevator dinged, *thank God,* and she stepped in. Before the doors closed, Jean Luc slipped inside with a smug look on his face.

She looked at the elevator panel as the red numbers counted down. *Twelve.* She was not going to ask him what the hell was going on. *Eleven.* It was not her business. *Ten.* "What was that all about? Did she give you her number?"

His grin widened. "Yes, she did."

She couldn't look at him. Her eyes zeroed in on the panel again. *Eight...Seven.* "And?" She turned and glared at him. "Do you think it's appropriate to be asking her for a date when we're trying to figure out who the killer is?"

His eyebrow shot up. "I will not be calling her for a date. She was massaging Renato with some type of oil. My hope is that Marty can extract the oil residue on her hands from this paper. We can then discover if it is a match to the oil found on Melanie."

"Oh." Her face heated and she looked back at the panel again. *Five.*

"Why would you care if I was flirting with the masseuse, Talia?"

Four. "I...I don't care. Not really. I just wanted to make sure you were being professional. That's all."

"You have nothing to worry about."

She glanced over at him, and if she wasn't mistaken, he was smirking. Smirking!

She glared at the panel again. *Two.* This was the longest damn elevator ride of her life.

Talia and Jean Luc parked in her driveway after dropping Will and Misha off at the lab. They were going to work with Marty for a while and then find something to eat. Again. Talia did not have the energy to watch Misha eat yet another time, so both she and Jean Luc declined. Now they were sitting awkwardly, staring at each other. Or she was sitting awkwardly. Jean Luc seemed calm and composed. His mood had changed for the better since their meeting with Renato. Or was it since she had made an ass out of herself in the elevator?

"Are you truly okay with me staying at your house, Talia?"

"Yes. Misha's right. I have the extra bedrooms, and since he's staying, it makes sense that you stay too."

Jean Luc followed her into the house, and she led him upstairs to the second bedroom. He set his duffle bag on the bed.

She hovered in the doorway.

Jean Luc turned and stared at her with his dark eyes. "Come in, Talia."

She hesitated.

"I will not bite." He paused. "Unless you wish me too."

CHAPTER 8

"Was that a joke, vampire?" Talia's eyes flashed gold.

Jean Luc struggled to suppress his smile. She was so beautiful she made him lose his train of thought. But he needed his wits about him to win her back. After her reaction in the elevator earlier, he knew in his vampire heart that not all hope was lost. She still had feelings for him. Still cared about him.

Then why was she pushing him away? She marched into the room quickly, as if to prove a point. Talia always stood up to a dare, and from the look in her eyes, she was going to push back, hard.

"Don't get used to running the investigation. I let you take lead with Renato because I thought you would get more out of him than I would."

Jean Luc inclined his head. "And I appreciate your trust in my investigative skills."

She frowned at him. "First humor and now sarcasm? Maybe Kyle is rubbing off on you."

He did not respond, knowing no matter what he said, she would attack.

"If Kyle had been here, she would have been right up in Renato's face."

"You are probably correct. But Kyle is not vampire. She is not subject to our laws, Talia. If you had confronted him, Renato could file a complaint against you with the council. Do you wish to lose your job?"

She grimaced. "He's slimy. He might not be the killer, but he's not innocent. When you told him about Melanie, he acted like she was no more important than a bug."

"Many of the founding vampires have been alive for so long that they have lost their capacity to feel empathy for those around them. They have no problem twisting the world to their version of the truth."

"Speaking of twisting the truth, what was with the lie earlier?"

He frowned. "What do you mean?"

"When Misha asked about your acquaintance, Leonardo, and you said he was a new recruit. I got the impression you weren't telling the truth. What didn't you want to say in front of everyone?"

She could sense he was lying? "It is not important."

"It's important enough that you lied to Misha about it."

"Leo would not be listed as working for *La Société* because he is an enforcer."

"He told you that?"

"Not directly, since they are not allowed to tell anyone, but that is his job."

"Jean Luc, he is serious business. Didn't you tell me that enforcers are the vamp version of the CIA? If *La Société* has sent an enforcer, then there will be bloodshed. And we'll be left to clean up the mess. Who is this Leo to you?"

Jean Luc closed his eyes for a moment. Memories bubbled just under the surface. Was he ready to let them out into the light of day? When he opened his eyes again, he looked at Talia. The fight had gone out of her stance, and her face was full of concern.

"Tell me what's wrong."

He sat on the foot of the bed, and she sat beside him.

"Leo and I met during The Wars. When I was turned and lost Jacqueline and my son, I wanted to kill myself. The vampires who worked for Pierre LeBlanc assigned Leo to watch over the newly turned."

She stiffened next to him. "Leo worked for them!"

"He had been forcibly turned himself."

"Then why was he helping them?"

"He was not helping them. Not really. He was trying to keep us alive. He hated LeBlanc and all he stood for, just as I did, but he was not willing to lie down and die. He saved me countless times on the battlefield. Times when I would have simply stood there and allowed myself to be struck down to stop the pain, he protected me."

Jean Luc's hands moved restlessly on his legs, and Talia reached for him, grasping one hand.

"One day he stepped in front of a sword meant for me. It would have taken his head off if I had not pushed him out of the way at the last second. He bears the scar on his neck to this day, and I do not know why. Unlike other scars, it never fully healed. Maybe it was because he had been so close to death. But he saved me. And I vowed I would do the same for him. I swore a blood oath to him."

Talia rubbed her thumb in slow circles over the back of his hand. He stared at their hands, folded together.

"What is a blood oath? You've never mentioned one before."

"It is not something that happens much anymore. When a vampire swears a blood oath to another, he ties himself to that vampire through blood. He promises to give his life for the other. If someone threatens Leo, I must either fight that person to the death or die in Leo's stead."

"Why would you let someone have that much power over you?"

Jean Luc placed his other hand on top of Talia's trapping it between both of his. "There is nothing to worry about, Talia. This is the first time I have seen Leo in more than one hundred years. And he has told me he will not hold me to it."

"But you still would do it anyway."

"*Oui*."

Jean Luc gazed into her gold-laced, brown eyes. He wanted to pull her to him and kiss her. Make her realize they were meant for each other. Her eyes widened as if she could read his thoughts. After a second, Jean Luc let her go and she stood.

He stood as well. "I am supposed to rendezvous with Leo tonight. I would like you to meet him."

"Of course. Where?"

He smiled slightly, attempting to lighten the mood. "Leo wants to watch the fountain show."

As usual, a crowd gathered around the hotel. It was almost time for the show to begin. Every half hour, the fountains drew tourists in droves to watch the water dance to music. Talia had been living in Vegas for years, and so many of the shows had become humdrum to her. But there was something magical about the fountains.

She stood next to Jean Luc and studied the crowd. Worn-out parents with cranky toddlers, couples dressed up for an evening out, hardcore gamblers not caring what they looked like as they moved from one hotel to the next.

She turned to Jean Luc. Her heart was still aching from their earlier discussion. He had survived so much in his lifetime, and his strength made her love him all the more. She caught her breath. She did love him. She did want to be with him. And she would tell him as much...as soon as they were alone.

Jean Luc pointed into the crowd at a tall male whose back was to them. "That is Leo."

They started toward him when Jean Luc's phone rang. He pulled it out and studied the screen. "It is Misha."

"Go ahead and get it. Maybe they have some news. I'll go introduce myself to Leo."

Jean Luc nodded and walked in the opposite direction, away from the noisy crowd.

Talia kept Leo in her sights. Tingling formed low and sharp in her spine. She jerked at the intensity of it. He must be a formidable vamp to be throwing off that much power when he wasn't even close yet. The static charged up her spine and coalesced in her brain, and she held her breath to keep herself from gasping. The music started, the water danced, and the crowd surged toward the show, pushing her closer to Leo.

The heat from him soaked into her. He turned. Her vision narrowed until the noise and the people around her disappeared. *No!*

She stared into the eyes of the devil himself — the son of a bitch who'd turned her.

CHAPTER 9

Talia struggled for calm. Terror fought for dominance over rage, making it hard to breathe.

Leo chuckled. "Oh, irony, you are both beautiful and twisted."

"You bastard," Talia hissed.

"Watch your language, Talia. There are children present."

As if in answer to his summons, a toddler bumped into his leg and fell down on his butt, then burst into tears. Leo bent and picked him up. A harried-looking woman stood a couple feet away and pushed her way over to them.

"Michael!"

Leo handed her the toddler, and she thanked him before returning to her husband's side.

Talia watched the interchange and willed her claws to retract. She could easily imagine herself ripping his throat out. She had the right, but not here, not now. There were too many vulnerabilities here. Too much risk of casualties.

She lowered her voice to a pitch only his vamp ears could hear. "Why are you here, Chris?"

"To stop a killer. It's an added bonus to see you again."

"A bonus? Everything about you is a lie. Even your name. Chris, Leo or whatever you call yourself."

"I did not lie to you. My full name is Leonardo Christophe Salazar."

"You turned me against my will and then left me. I had no idea what I had become. No one to teach me what it meant to be a vampire."

He shrugged. "And yet you survived. From the looks of it, very well, my beautiful girl."

"Don't ever call me that again." Hate sizzled under her skin at his flippant response. "I'm going to kill you."

He wagged his finger at her as if she were a small child. "Ah, ah, ah, Talia. I would watch what I say."

"Why the hell should I? I promise you. You. Are. Dead."

"I don't think Jean Luc would like to hear you threaten me."

"Why the hell would he care...?" Her throat closed on the words. *Oh God.*

He smiled. "I see he has told you about the oath. Would you like to tell me again how you plan to kill me?"

No!

"Now watch what you say, my beautiful girl. He's coming this way. I wouldn't want to be forced to invoke the oath."

Talia took a deep breath and pulled in all of her energy — all the rage and frustration — and locked them away.

Jean Luc walked up and grasped Leo's forearm in a handshake of old. "I see you have met Talia."

Leo smiled. "I have, and she is as amazing as you said."

Jean Luc's eyes widened at his words, but when he

turned to Talia, they narrowed on her face. "Is something wrong?"

"No. Nothing's wrong."

"Are you sure?"

"Yes." She didn't dare look at Chris again. "I...just need to feed. What did Misha have to say?"

"Both Misha and Marty have been busy. It looks more and more like Renato may be guilty. We need to go to the lab. Do you wish to come along, Leo?"

Talia held her breath, waiting.

"I do not want to stray too far away from the contingent. They are acting a little too skittish. Maybe your earlier meeting with Renato has made him nervous."

Jean Luc shrugged. "Stay close to him then, and let us know if he attempts to leave Vegas."

Chris bowed slightly. "Of course. It was a pleasure to meet you, Talia."

She bit the inside of her lip to stop from spewing what she really wanted to say to him. She nodded instead, and he turned and walked away.

Jean Luc stared hard at her for a moment. "We will stop and get you some blood first. You do not look right to me."

She shrugged. She might never be right again.

CHAPTER 10

Something was wrong with Talia. Jean Luc observed her closely. Even after feeding, she still seemed off. Her mouth was pinched and her eyes had lost their glorious spark. Had he pushed her too hard? Had he scared her away with the maudlin talk of his past?

They had just arrived at the lab, and Misha, Will, and Marty were clearly bursting to tell them some sort of news.

"Okay, guys what have you got?" Talia sighed.

Marty started. "The oil residue on the paper Jean Luc gave me is the same oil as I found on Melanie Thomas."

"So it is Renato," Jean Luc responded.

Talia shook her head. "Or the masseuse. It could be anyone in his contingent. It could be Vamp One or Vamp Two, for all we know."

Misha's eyebrow lifted. "Vamp One or Vamp Two? Are we in a paranormal Dr. Seuss now?"

Talia didn't crack a smile. "They are Renato's guards."

Will interjected, "So we have enough evidence to start questioning the entire group. Someone is bound to slip up. We can narrow it down by finding out who was away from the contingent on the night of Melanie's murder."

Misha cocked his head. "I have been doing some searching and found something interesting as well. Renato is not the only founding vampire on the move. Three others from Europe and one from China have recently arrived in the United States."

"Where are they?" Talia asked.

"Spread out in various cities, but the odds against having all these founding vamps here at one time are astronomical."

"Why would they come here?" Marty asked.

There could be only one reason, but it made Jean Luc's heart thud. "A tribunal."

Talia inhaled sharply, and Misha gave a low whistle.

Will looked between them. "Explain to the rest of us what you mean."

"A tribunal is called when our head vampire's rule is challenged. Only founding vampires can challenge our ruler."

"Does this happen a lot?"

"There has not been a challenge in over three hundred years."

"So they're going to New York, then?" Marty asked. "Doesn't your leader live in New York City?"

"Tobias lives in New York, but they won't challenge him on his home territory. They will use last year's fiasco with Sebastian and his murder spree as their excuse to challenge him. They will argue that a good leader would have not allowed the murders to occur. Therefore, they will want to interrogate everyone involved. Which means it will take place in Cleveland."

Misha sighed. "I'll contact the pilot to see when we

can head back. Is there still time for Will to take me to get all-you-can-eat crab legs?"

Talia frowned. "We're not going anywhere. Renato and his followers are still here, and we have a murderer to catch."

She stalked out of the room.

Silence reigned until Will spoke. "Damn. She's pissed about something. Maybe I should go talk to her."

Jean Luc stepped in front of him. "No. Let me try." He walked out of the lab and found Talia standing outside, gazing up at the moon.

"Talia, what is wrong?

"Nothing."

"Are you sure?"

"I'm fine, Jean Luc. Just pissed at our species for believing we have the right to destroy someone weaker."

"I know this must bring back bad memories of your turning."

She spun around to glower at him. "Why would you say that?"

"Because I am not sure whether you were talking about you or Melanie. Luckily, you survived."

"Maybe she was the lucky one."

His fangs elongated, and a growl erupted from his chest. "Never say that again."

She stumbled back from him. "I need some time by myself, Jean Luc."

"That is not a good idea."

"Tough. Now back off."

He opened his mouth to protest.

"Please, Jean Luc. Just give me some time. You're right; this case is getting to me."

He nodded, and she flashed away. He waited a few

seconds, and then flashed after her. He would give her some space, but he needed to watch over her. Something was not right.

And it scared him.

Talia opened her mind, searching for Chris. He was her sire by blood, if nothing else, so she should be able to locate him. She ended up standing in the alley next to The Cosmo hotel. Chris had been there recently, but the tingling sensation was light. It made sense that he would be staying close to the contingent. She would wait for him.

She needed a plan. If she attacked him when Jean Luc was not around, he would never need to know she was the one who had killed Chris. And he would be unable to invoke the oath. But she couldn't kill him on the strip. Someone else could be hurt in the crossfire. She needed time to think and plan.

Three hours of lurking in an alley, and Talia had reached her limit. She stalked into the hotel toward the door behind the reservation counter. Veronique stood there, a scowl souring her face.

"Have the vamps from Europe checked out?" Talia asked.

"They left hours ago."

"Going where?"

"I don't know."

Talia took a step toward her. "They didn't have you arrange transport?"

Veronique huffed. "They went to the airport."

"And did you happen to hear where they were going?"

"I don't make a point of listening in on private conversations."

Talia glared at her.

"Fine! They were going to *Cleveland*, of all places."

Veronique actually shuddered after saying the word. Talia gripped her hands behind her back to keep from slapping the French Barbie doll and turned on her heel. She dialed her phone while she hustled out the hotel doors.

"Hope you got your fill of crab legs, Misha. It's time to fire up the jet."

CHAPTER 11

Jean Luc glanced toward the back of the plane, where Talia sat alone. Her eyes were closed, and she wore earbuds hooked to her phone. Her music blared loud enough for him to hear it, even this far away.

When he had followed her, she had simply gone to The Cosmopolitan and stood outside for hours. If she wanted to shut him out for now, he would cooperate, but he would find out what was bothering her soon.

"Oh, boy." Will mumbled. "She's listening to rap. That's not a good sign."

"Why?" Jean Luc asked.

"T is normally pretty laid back. But when she does get upset, she listens to music. I can gauge how upset she is by the type of music. Slightly irritated, and she listens to alternative. Mad, and she gravitates to reggae. Majorly pissed, she listens to rap, and if that happens, I make myself scarce."

Misha chuckled. "You know her well."

Will shrugged. "She's my partner. We have each other's back."

Jean Luc clenched his fists. "So you are close."

Will stared at him for a moment before answering. "She's not just my partner, she's my friend."

"Are you sleeping with her?" Misha blurted.

Mon Dieu! Jean Luc just barely stopped himself from groaning.

"Are you sleeping with Jean Luc?" Will countered.

Misha chuckled. "No. He is not my type. Too moody."

Will smiled then looked straight at Jean Luc before answering. "I am not sleeping with her. We're friends. Not that she isn't drop-dead gorgeous, but nothing has ever happened or will happen between us."

"And why is that?" Jean Luc asked before he could stop himself.

"Because she's in love with someone else and is too stubborn to admit it. Get the picture?"

"*Oui.*"

"That reminds me of someone else I know," Misha quipped.

Jean Luc narrowed his eyes at him.

Misha's responding chuckle erupted into a belly laugh.

Jean Luc pulled the van out of long-term parking, tires screeching as he turned in the direction of the airport exit.

"Holy crap! Is driving like a maniac part of the vampire handbook?" Will asked.

"Most definitely," Misha answered.

"T drives the same way."

Jean Luc looked in the rearview mirror at Talia. He wanted her to chime in to the conversation and put both males in their places. Instead, she sat quietly looking out the window. "Misha, have we heard from Dolly?"

Misha checked his phone. "She emailed me. Renato's contingent is staying at the Renaissance. Why do you think your friend Leo hasn't contacted you yet?"

"Good question," Talia interjected.

Jean Luc pulled his phone out of his pocket and handed it to Misha. "Maybe he did while we were on the plane."

Misha nodded. "Yep there's a text here."

"What does it say?" Talia asked.

"Says he followed group to Cleveland. He'll contact Jean Luc with more details."

"So where to first?" Will asked.

"Now that we can trace the oil to Renato, we need to question him and the contingent again," Jean Luc said.

Misha's phone rang, and he hit the speaker button. "Hello, little one."

"You guys back in town yet?" Kyle's voice was easy to hear.

"Yes, we are in the van heading to the Renaissance to interrogate some vampires."

"Were you going to call me?"

"I didn't want to interrupt anything between you and Griffin. You both need some alone time."

"Griffin's having to deal with some pack business. I'm free and ready to help. I'll meet you at the hotel. How's Jean Luc doing? Has he gotten anywhere with Talia yet?"

Misha punched the speaker button off and put the phone to his ear. "You were on speaker just now."

The expletive that exploded through the phone was

loud enough that even Will in the far back seat laughed.

"We'll see you in a few minutes, Kyle."

"What are we waiting for?" Talia asked, looking around the lobby.

Jean Luc answered, "Kyle should be here any minute. We can then start interviewing contingent members. Dolly emailed Misha the members' room numbers.

"I have already emailed them to your phones," Misha added.

They were wasting time. The sooner they figured out who the killer was, the sooner she could deal with Chris. "Besides Renato, we have ten others to interview. We should split up and start questioning the group."

Jean Luc nodded. "I agree. Misha and Will, you work together and—"

"I'll take Kyle," Talia interrupted.

"You'll take me where?" Kyle asked as she sauntered up to the group.

Will smiled. "Hey, Kyle."

Talia turned to her. "We're splitting up to interrogate people. You're with me. We'll take the first four names on the list Dolly sent." She headed for the elevator.

"All righty, then," Kyle replied and jogged up next to her. "Good to see you again, too."

Talia hit the elevator button and the doors slid open. "We're questioning vampires who are suspects in a murder. Let me do the talking."

Kyle smiled. "You sound like Jean Luc."

"But unlike Jean Luc, I mean it when I say let me do the talking."

Kyle's smile dimmed. "Yes, your Vampiredness, whatever you say. If you're that worried I'm going to screw things up, then why did you ask to be paired with me?"

Talia didn't answer. Instead, she focused on the floor numbers clicking past. *Two.*

After a few seconds, Kyle chuckled. "You didn't want to be alone with Jean Luc, right? It's like junior high all over again but with fangs."

Talia ignored her. *Three.*

"Sometimes I wish that, instead of changing memories, my power could change attitudes. Now that would be a cool gift to have. People acting pissy around you, and you just zap them and they're happy. Yep, that would be a cool power."

Four.

This was the second longest damn elevator ride of her life.

Forty-five minutes later, they were no closer to finding the killer. She and Kyle had interviewed four vamps who, unless they were very good actors, had no clue what was going on, and they all had an alibi for the night Melanie was attacked.

Talia marched toward the elevator with Kyle on her heels. At the last minute, she veered through the door leading to the stairs. Something was drawing her that way. A tingling so slight it could have been her imagination. Or maybe she simply didn't want a repeat of the elevator ride up with Kyle.

"Well, that was a bust. Hopefully the guys are having better luck."

Talia stopped on the stairs. "Quiet."

Kyle stopped next to her, hands on her hips. "I've had it. What the hell is your problem?"

"No, listen."

A soft moan echoed up the stairwell. Talia looked over the handrail and saw a woman lying on the landing two floors down. The faint scent of blood reached her. Talia flashed down the stairs and stopped next to the woman. She was young, maybe college age, with long blond hair flopped over to cover her face. Her arms and legs were held close to her body in the fetal position.

Talia squatted, and the girl flinched at her closeness, throwing an arm up over her face. Her forearm had several fang marks running along it.

"I won't hurt you. I'm here to help."

Kyle ran down the stairs, and when the girl flinched again, Talia held up her hand to stop Kyle from coming any closer. Talia's heart ached. *Who would do this?*

"You're safe now. Let me help you."

The girl lifted her head, and her hair fell back from her face. She opened her eyes and stared at Talia for a moment. Her expression was blank. Shock. They needed to get her out of here.

"I'm Talia. Can you tell me your name?"

The girl blinked at her, and her eyes lost some of their haziness. "Annie."

"Okay, Annie. Will you allow me to check you over?"

She nodded, and Talia quickly examined her. She had bites on both arms and her neck.

"Do you think you can stand?"

Annie nodded again, and Talia held out her hand to offer her help up.

The girl grabbed Talia's hand, and her eyes flashed red. *Shit!* Annie yanked Talia toward her, Talia lost her balance, and Annie bit her hard in the neck, ripping at her throat. Talia pushed against her chest, but the girl was surprisingly strong.

Kyle yelled and ran to the door leading out of the stairwell. *Where the hell was she going?*

After a few more harsh pulls, Talia's vision went fuzzy. The other vamp must have hit her jugular. "Let go, Annie!"

Kyle ran back with something metallic in her hands. "Let her go!"

White foam sprayed them, and Annie jerked away from Talia's neck. When Annie lunged for her neck again, Kyle swung the cylinder at the girl. A metallic *thunk* echoed through the stairwell. Then another *thunk*.

Talia's eyelids fluttered and then closed.

CHAPTER 12

Jean Luc rubbed the back of his neck while he waited in the lobby for the others to arrive. He was no closer to figuring out who the killer was. Renato and his guards were not in the building. According to Renato's secretary, he was at an appointment he had set up himself, which meant she did not have any details. And based on her irritation, Jean Luc was convinced it was not a common occurrence. Maybe Renato was meeting with the other founding vampires to prepare for the tribunal.

Misha and Will walked up to him.

"No luck, my friend?" Misha asked.

"No. You?"

"No." Misha slapped Will on the shoulder. "This reminds me of an episode from *Law and Order*. The cops couldn't narrow down the killer because there were so many suspects."

Jean Luc's spine tingled. Something wasn't right. He looked around the lobby to try and pinpoint where the sensation came from.

Misha stopped rambling about his television show and gave Jean Luc a hard look. "What is it, my friend?"

"I do not know. I—"

Pain! He jerked. *Mon Dieu, Talia.*

Misha grabbed his arm. "Jean Luc!"

"Talia, she—" He pulled out of Misha's grip and ran toward the back of the hotel.

Where was she? He stopped for a second and concentrated. She was above him. The elevator was too slow. Where was the stairwell?

He stopped himself from flashing in front of the hotel guests, instead ran down the hall and pushed open the door to the stairs.

Kyle's shout echoed from above. "Let her go!"

He flashed up the empty stairs until he reached the third-floor landing. Kyle sprayed a fire extinguisher at a fledgling vampire who was ravaging Talia's neck. Before Jean Luc could flash again, Kyle swung the extinguisher hard against the vampire's head.

Kyle didn't take a breath before she swung the extinguisher with all her might again, knocking the vampire across the floor.

Jean Luc bared his fangs and stood between the fledgling, Talia, and Kyle.

A door slammed open from below. Within seconds, Will and Misha thundered up the stairs.

"Shit!" Will exclaimed, reaching for Talia.

Jean Luc growled. *Non! Mine.*

Misha grabbed Will's arm. "Don't touch her, Will. Take care of the vamp, and let Jean Luc help her."

Will's eyes widened when he glanced at Jean Luc. "Okay."

While Will and Misha grabbed the fledgling and handcuffed her, Jean Luc started to breathe again. He flashed to Talia, yanked his coat off, and then his shirt, which he used to wipe the blood and foam away from her neck. Blood gushed from the wound, and he clamped his hand over her skin and bent, holding the tear together and licking her throat. *Stop the bleeding.*

Stop the bleeding. Why was it taking so long? The chemicals in his saliva should help seal the wound.

After a few minutes, her neck was partially healed, but she still lay limp in his arms. She had lost a lot of blood. He wanted to see her eyes open and sparking with flecks of gold.

"Jean Luc."

He would need to feed her soon. Otherwise, it would take days or even weeks for her to heal.

"Jean Luc!"

He looked up at Kyle, and she smiled, even though her eyes were tight with worry.

"Misha is pulling the van around back. We can go down the stairs and out that way."

He glanced around the landing and realized they were the only ones there. When had Misha and Will taken the fledgling away?

"She's going to be okay?" Kyle asked.

"*Oui.*"

Kyle let out a hard breath. "Good." She pulled her coat off. "Wrap this around her to hide the blood on her clothes. And put your own coat back on. We can't have you prancing around shirtless. Women will swoon."

Jean Luc let out his own shaky breath and complied with Kyle's orders. Then he lifted Talia and walked carefully down the stairs. He tucked Talia's head against his chest, where it belonged. She would be all right, and they would be together again.

He would see to it.

CHAPTER 13

Talia couldn't open her eyes. *So tired.*

She didn't know where she was. But she did know she was safe. Jean Luc's scent surrounded her, as did his words, first English, then French, telling her she would be fine. She ached, needing something. A wrist pressed against her lips, and liquid warmth invaded her mouth. It tasted like citrus and spice, like life and power. She lapped her tongue over the skin, and then began to suckle.

She didn't know how long she fed, but eventually, the wrist was removed, and the words came back, telling her to rest. She faded again, but not before lips lightly touched her forehead.

She woke to the sound of a heartbeat. No, it was two heartbeats. Hers and…she turned her head to the right. Jean Luc sat in a chair in the corner of the room. When he saw she was watching him, he stood and stepped up to the bed.

"How are you feeling?"

She took a deep breath. "I'm fine."

His gaze narrowed on her, as if judging the truth of her statement. "Do you remember what happened?"

"Annie attacked me. Is she okay?"

"Doc is with her. We have her sedated. She was

very upset when she realized what she had done to you."

"We're at the BSR facility?"

"Yes. Why did you risk going near the fledgling? You know how dangerous a newly turned vampire can be."

"She was hurt, and I didn't sense that she had just been turned."

"Right now she is feral. Hopefully once things are explained to her she will get a handle on her hunger."

Talia *should* have known better, but her emotions had blinded her. "I thought Annie had been attacked like Melanie. I needed to help her."

Jean Luc placed his hand on her arm. "It is midafternoon. You have been asleep since this morning. You are healing, but slower than normal since you lost a lot of blood."

"You've been feeding me."

He nodded, and she frowned. If she couldn't even defend herself from a fledgling, how would she face Chris?

Jean Luc removed his hand from her arm. "There was no time to ask your permission, Talia. It would have taken weeks for you to rebuild your blood supply without my help."

"No. I'm not upset about that. Thank you for helping me. What are our next steps?"

"Renato and his guards have gone missing. We must find him before he strikes again."

Talia shook her head. "Something's not right about this, Jean Luc. Why would Renato attack her? And in the same hotel where he's staying? Why would he want to bring trouble knocking at his own door right before he was involved in a tribunal? It doesn't make sense."

"Maybe he has gone mad."

"Or maybe someone is setting him up? Someone in his contingent?" She sat up in the bed. "Or one of the other founding vampires?"

"To what end?" Jean Luc asked.

"If the tribunal is called, how is a new leader chosen?"

"Several founding vampires must allege misconduct on the part of the leader, and if he is removed, then those vampires are vetted as candidates for the new leader."

"Renato is in the running for this, right? What if one of the other founders wants to make sure he is not chosen? Right now, he doesn't look like a good choice after what's been happening."

"You have a point. But I still need to speak with Renato."

"So go look for him."

He hesitated, and she smiled.

"I'm fine, honest. I'll be good and stay here and rest. But I'm out of this bed tomorrow morning. Do we have a deal?"

"We have a deal. Are you up for visitors while I am gone?"

He didn't fool her. Visitors meant someone to watch over her, but she wouldn't fight him on that either. "Yes."

Jean Luc walked toward the door, and she called out to him, "Don't go after Renato alone."

He looked over his shoulder, his lips turning up slightly. "I thought you said it was not him?"

She opened her mouth to argue, and he continued, "Misha would not let me go alone even if I chose to. But he will want to see you before we go, so I will send him in."

Five minutes later, Misha and Will bustled into the room.

Will grabbed her hand. "You doin' okay, T?"

"Yes. Thanks."

Misha grinned. "You scared me, my dear. Don't do that again."

"Yes, sir. Has anyone talked to Annie yet?"

"Nope," Will answered. "She's sedated. Since she's having issues with bloodlust, Doc suggested I shouldn't get too close, since shifter blood is so yummy to you vamps and all."

Talia rolled her eyes. "That ego of yours is going to get you into trouble one of these days, Will."

Will motioned to Misha. "Maybe Mr. Stinky Blood here can talk to her."

"My blood is not stinky!" Misha sputtered. "It's not palatable to vampires, which I personally think is a good thing. The fledgling is not too happy with *either* of us, since we cuffed her and brought her here."

"Well, what about Kyle?"

Will and Misha shook their heads at the same time.

Will spoke up first. "Annie won't let Kyle near her. I don't blame her. Kyle let her have it."

Talia frowned. She couldn't remember exactly what happened, just snippets of Kyle shouting. "What did she do?"

Misha cut in. "It was brilliant. Shades of the show *Alias*. Sydney Bristow would be proud. She grabbed a fire extinguisher and sprayed Annie to shock her into letting you go. Then she walloped her with the canister. Twice."

Will chuckled. "If Kyle wasn't dating the leader of the shifters, I would so go after her."

"I owe her my thanks." Talia said.

Misha leaned down and kissed her on top of her

head. "Kyle will be in to visit in a little bit. Close your eyes for a while and rest."

"I'm not tired."

"You know I'll keep arguing with you until you agree, yes?"

"Stubborn Russian. Fine. I'll rest if you watch out for Jean Luc."

Misha's eyes narrowed on her. "Always."

Will squeezed her hand before following Misha out of the room.

Talia closed her eyes. She wasn't tired. She would just close them for a few minutes.

Talia opened her eyes. Once again, she was not alone in the room. Kyle sat in the chair Jean Luc had vacated.

"How are you feeling?"

"Great."

Kyle stood and walked closer to the bed. "*Right.*"

Talia ignored her tone. "How long was I asleep?"

"Two hours."

"How is Annie doing?"

"Doc is the only person she'll let near her without freaking out, and she's not really talking to her either. I wish I could help."

"You can't make her forget, Kyle. She's a vampire now. Everything she does has consequences. Have we heard anything from the guys?"

"Just that they're still looking for Renato."

"I understand from Misha and Will that you're pretty handy with a fire extinguisher."

"I felt bad for a split second, but then I thought, eh, she'll heal."

"She'll heal from the extinguisher, but it will take a long time before she heals from the forced turning."

"It sounds like you speak from experience." Kyle held up her hands. "And before you go postal, Jean Luc didn't tell me anything about your past. Your reactions are like a neon sign."

Talia fisted her hands before her claws extended. "I was turned by force. It's like a form of rape. A violation. A taking away of my humanity."

"I'm sorry some S.O.B. thought he could do that to you."

"I've moved forward, but I'll never forget."

"Is the bastard who turned you still alive?"

Her nerves tingled in alarm, but Kyle didn't look like she knew anything. "I believe so."

"I hope he gets what's coming to him."

Talia nodded, her throat too tight to make a sound. He would get what was coming to him. She would see to it.

———————

Jean Luc read the text from Kyle and took a deep breath. Talia was doing well. He stood in an alley down the street from the hotel, waiting for Leo to show up. He had practically threatened Misha with bodily injury to get the demon to let him meet with Leo alone.

Moments later, Leo appeared and stood before him. "Jean Luc."

"Do you know where Renato is?"

"I see we are going to dispense with the pleasantries tonight. I believe he is meeting with Jia Li."

"The founding vampire from Beijing?"

"Yes."

"So they must be planning a tribunal."

"That's what it looks like to me. But take heart. With the recent stain on Renato's reputation, he won't be ruling us."

"I am not convinced he is guilty."

"You're sticking up for Renato now?"

"Talia does not believe Renato is responsible, and I agree with her. Why would he risk something like this so close to the tribunal?"

"Because he doesn't believe rules are meant for him?"

"Perhaps."

"Do you miss the old days Jean Luc?"

Jean Luc raised his eyebrows in question.

"Oh, I don't mean The Wars. I mean the simpler times. What happened to solving disagreements with a few punches? Now we call attorneys or spread gossip through social media. Is this what we fought for?"

Jean Luc thought for a moment before responding. "I think that what is truly important never changes. And we have to fight to preserve it in whatever way is necessary."

Leo frowned slightly before grinning at him. "Spoken like a besotted fool. I'll get in touch with you when I know more about Renato." He walked out of the alley.

Jean Luc stared at his retreating back until he was alone. He might be besotted, but he was no fool. Four hundred years had taught him very few things really mattered in this world. And when you found the one who did, you held on tight.

CHAPTER 14

Talia stood outside Annie's room, staring through the rectangular door window. Annie huddled in a ball on the bed.

Talia clicked the lock, and Annie jerked, her eyes widening when Talia walked into the room. Talia stayed by the door so as not to stress her out and to maintain space between them in case the fledgling tried to attack again. Annie's fledgling scent permeated the air. It reminded Talia of freshly washed linens. Why she hadn't sensed it in the stairwell where she found Annie was a mystery to her.

"How are you feeling, Annie?"

"Okay."

"I don't know if you remember me from earlier today?"

Annie nodded and looked away. "I'm so...I don't know what happened...I never meant to hurt you."

"It's okay."

"How can you say that?" She blinked, and a tear rolled down her cheek. "After what I did to you? I'm a monster."

"No. You're a vampire."

She gasped. "That's crazy. They're not real."

"How else can you explain what happened?"

"I can't. Maybe I have some virus. Or maybe *I'm* just crazy."

"We want to help you. What do you remember from this morning? Before I found you."

"I was at the hotel bar last night." She looked down at her hands. "I was trying to pick someone up. My friends told me if I was looking for a one-night stand, I should go to a nice hotel and sit in the bar."

"And did you meet someone?"

"Yes."

"Do you remember his name or what he looks like?"

She frowned. "No, it's blurry. Why would he be blurry?"

"He made you forget."

"He can do that?"

"What about his voice — did he have an accent?"

"No. He sounded normal. Like you and me. He..." She stopped and rubbed her temples.

"What is it, Annie?"

"He called me something."

"Can you remember?"

"Yes. He called me his *beautiful girl*." Tears rolled down her face. "He told me if I was a good girl he wouldn't kill me like the other one."

Talia's throat closed, and she struggled for air. Chris. It was Chris. All of it. Melanie *and* Annie. Talia was going to kill him. *Damn.* She should have killed him before. And now Annie had to suffer because of her.

"Are you okay, Talia?"

God, Annie was trying to comfort her? "Yes. I'm fine. Why don't you rest for a while? I'll come check on you later."

She stepped out of the room and locked the door. It would be dark soon. She would hunt him then and kill him for what he had done to Melanie and Annie. What he had done to her.

Talia ran down the corridor to her room. Someone had left her bag in the room and she pulled out fresh clothes. Before she could take off the hospital scrubs, tingling ran down her spine. *Not now!* Jean Luc was back. He would stop her. She couldn't tell him the truth. He would go after Chris and die because of that damn blood oath.

"What are you doing, Talia?"

She turned to him and smiled. "I was going to take a shower and then change into something else."

"You are feeling stronger?"

"I feel great. Have you found Renato yet?"

"No. I spoke with Leo. Renato is meeting with Jia Li."

She stopped herself from gasping at his name. She had to keep Chris away from Jean Luc.

She stared at his face, into his dark eyes. She loved him. Had never stopped, but now she had to leave him again. Had to protect him from her mistakes. From her stupidity in trusting Chris and then not telling Jean Luc the truth.

He stepped forward and laid his hand on her cheek. "When this is over, Talia, let us renew our discussion, this time with honesty."

And for once, the emotions on his face, in his eyes, were front and center. He wanted her. If she were noble, she would walk away now. But she couldn't do that, either. She wanted to hold him and be with him one last time. She was selfish, but she was already damned, so she had nothing left to lose.

"Talia. Are you okay?"

She placed her fingers over his lips. "Please. I don't want to talk. I need you. Can you do that? Can you be with me?" *One last time.*

He froze for a moment, staring hard at her. Was he going to back away? He opened his mouth, and she started to lift her fingers away, but he grabbed her wrist and held it to his lips. She gasped when he ran his tongue along her fingertips and sucked them into his mouth.

Warmth shot up her arm and filled her chest. His eyes flashed red, and when he finally opened his mouth to release her fingers, she could see his fangs were fully extended. He was the most gorgeous male—human or supernatural—she had ever seen.

"I have missed you, Talia."

"I've missed you, too."

She leaned forward and brushed her lips over his. So soft, so perfect, as if their lips were made to be pressed together. Two pieces to a puzzle. No. She couldn't think about what they could have had, what could have been. This would be her goodbye to him. In the future, when he thought of her, hopefully he would remember this moment instead of her betrayal.

Jean Luc's lips tingled. Actually tingled where they met Talia's. He thought he had remembered what it felt like to hold her, to make love to her. He had played it over and over again in his mind. But the reality was so much more delicious than his memories.

He leaned back and looked at her face. At her eyes sparking gold. "Are you sure you are well enough for this?"

She smiled, and it was like a siren call, and he was lost in a turbulent sea.

"I'm fine. Your blood healed me."

She licked up his jaw and nipped his earlobe, and he groaned aloud like an inexperienced virgin. She chuckled and ran her hands down his arms, grasping his hands with her own before tugging him toward the bed.

He stopped, and a sadness filled her eyes, as if she expected him to turn away. He kissed her hard, and then let go of her hands to walk to the door. He pulled the door blinds and locked it.

"Visitors would be unwelcome at the moment."

He flashed to her, grabbing her around the waist. She laughed and rested her hands on either side of his face. Talia kissed him again, but this time the softness was replaced with hunger and passion as their tongues danced together.

They fell on the bed, a tangle of limbs and wet kisses.

"Help me get out of these scrubs."

The claw on his index finger suddenly appeared, and he sliced down the center of the top and then the pants. Within seconds, she lay naked before him, and blood surged through his body like lava. She was his once again, and he was not about to let her go.

He stroked his lips along her neck to her pulse point, where he kissed and suckled lightly. Her lavender fragrance enveloped him, but he would not bite her tonight. She was still not fully recovered, and he would not risk it. But soon, he would once again draw her blood into his mouth and into his soul.

His lips traveled south, and when he teased her nipple, she moaned. She reached for his shirt and yanked it over his head. He stood for a moment and divested himself of the rest of his clothes. Her gaze felt like a physical caress as it moved over him. She held out her hand, and he grasped it, crawling over her.

He wanted to worship her slowly. But all thoughts of languid exploration evaporated when she ran her hand down his length and steered him to her. It had been too long, and he wanted her too much. He slid inside her in one stroke and held himself against her. Perfectly still. Willing his heart to beat in rhythm with hers so there was only one heartbeat between them.

Only then did he finally begin to move.

CHAPTER 15

Talia hurried down the hall. She had slipped away from Jean Luc, her mission clear. It was time to end this with Chris.

"Talia?"

She hung her head at the sound of his voice.

"Where are you going?"

She turned and faced him. He had dressed again, although his shirt was open, his chest and stomach on glorious display. "To get some air, Jean Luc."

His eyes narrowed on her, as if trying to unlock her secrets. "Why do you insist on being alone? On pushing me away?"

"I needed you tonight. But we can't go back again, Jean Luc. You have to let me go." She swallowed. "When this case is over, I'm leaving. Don't make this any harder than it needs to be."

He opened his mouth to argue, but she held up her hand. "Please. Go find Renato and figure out who is doing this before someone else gets hurt."

His face shuttered, all emotions wiped away. He nodded and walked past her.

She closed her eyes. Her breathing hitched. He would be safe, and that's what mattered. She would not let him die for her.

Hands clapped, and she opened her eyes to see Kyle standing at the end of the hall.

"That performance deserves an Oscar."

"What do you want, Kyle?"

Kyle marched over and leaned in close. "Why are you shutting him out?"

Talia had no time for this. "That's none of your business."

"That's where you're wrong. You're hurting him, Talia. And I won't tolerate that."

Talia stepped even closer. "*You* will not tolerate it? What do you intend to do?"

Kyle shook her head. "Oh, I know you could gut me where I stand, Miz Tough Vampire. But you won't."

"How can you be so sure?"

"Because Jean Luc wouldn't love someone who could do that to his family."

Talia froze.

"For some reason you're lying to him. You have some misguided need to protect him right now. I get it. I *was* you, pushing everyone away and lying to protect them."

Talia shook her head. "You have no idea what you're talking about."

"I have no idea what your problem is, because you won't tell us, but I know what I'm talking about. Let us help you. Let Jean Luc help you before you push him away for good."

Talia didn't respond.

Kyle stared for a moment, but when the silence stretched on, she turned and walked into a room. She shut the door with a definitive click.

———

Talia stood on the hotel rooftop and closed her eyes. Jean Luc had once told her a vampire could track their sire if they tried hard enough. That the link between sire and vampire was strong enough to make it possible. And Talia was all about the possible.

A light tickle ran along her spine into her brain, and she turned to the south. It was as if a thread of sensation twisted around her arms and legs and drew her like a marionette toward Chris. But he would not be her puppet master. She would be in control, and she would end this before anyone else was hurt.

She flashed along the quiet streets. Downtown Cleveland at night was not a popular area in late February. Talia stopped, her breath drifting around her in frigid waves. She was getting closer. The energy string now felt more like a thin rope wrapped around her wrists. She flashed again and found herself along the river leading out into Lake Erie. In front of her were several buildings that looked like out-of-business bars and restaurants.

She stopped in front of one with a large window overlooking the water. The tingling had turned into a roar of heat in her brain. He was powerful, but she couldn't back down now. Besides, he already knew she was here.

Talia pushed open the door. It wasn't much warmer inside, but at least the building protected her from the wind. She turned slowly to examine the room. Upturned chairs sat on tables covered with dust. A bar ran along the far wall with barstools sitting in a neat row, as if waiting for customers to return.

A whimper sounded from behind the bar. Talia stepped slowly, her breath stuttering when she caught the fresh linen scent. She stepped around the bar. Annie was crouched down in the corner.

"Annie? How did you get here?"

She hiccupped a sob. "He found me."

Jesus. There was no time to ask for details. She pulled Annie to her feet. "Where is he now?"

"I…I don't know."

"I'm right here, Talia."

Talia spun toward the door and stepped in front of Annie. "Stay behind me."

Chris walked toward the bar. "Are you going to protect her from me, Talia? A little late, don't you think?"

A sultry chuckle sounded behind her, and dread shot along Talia's nerve endings. Annie stepped around her toward Chris. Talia stared in shock as Annie's scent changed. Her fresh linen aroma morphed into something spicy.

"I'm so glad that's over. It's exhausting playing the damaged ingénue."

Chris reached for Annie and pulled her close. She rubbed herself wantonly against him while Talia's skin crawled.

"Talia, you've already met Annie, my wonderful actress. She had you fooled, did she not? When I turned her twenty-five years ago, this remarkable female surprised me. She is still able to pretend she is newly turned when the need arises. It is a unique power."

"Why, Chris?" Talia asked.

"You need to be more specific, my dear. Why what?"

"Why did you kill Melanie?"

Chris stroked Annie's chin, and she closed her eyes and practically purred. "I need beauty around me. Melanie was gorgeous. She would have made a glorious vampire. Unfortunately, I allowed Annie to taste her, and she got a bit carried away, didn't you, my beautiful girl?"

Annie smiled and batted her eyes like a heroine from a silent movie.

Talia shook her head. "She didn't *accidentally* take too much. She killed her on purpose. You didn't want the competition, did you? Someone who was prettier than you attracting Chris's eye. That wasn't something you could risk."

Annie glared at her. "You're just jealous because he kept me and threw you away."

Talia ignored her, directing her next words to Chris. "Why the production?"

"When I saw you again after all these years, I couldn't believe it. I thought you had died that day, but yet there you stood in front of me, swearing vengeance. And it made my blood race. Finally, a challenge! A new game to play. And I lobbed the first ball at you, telling you of Jean Luc's oath to me. Instead of lobbing the ball back, you backed away altogether. You were willing to throw it all away to protect him."

"So you lobbed a bigger ball at me."

Chris grinned. "What could I throw at you that would force your hand? Make you come after me even if it meant Jean Luc's life? A victim who had been turned the way I turned you. Someone who would remind you of what I had done to you."

Annie curtsied. "That would be me."

"Did you tell her to drain me as well?"

Chris's eyes widened at the question.

Anna smiled. "I improvised. I wouldn't have killed her, of course. That fun I left for you."

"You sultry minx!" He grabbed her around the waist, and she giggled when he growled at her.

Talia took a deep breath and swallowed the acid that surged up into her throat. They were both psychotic.

"So now what, Chris? You kill me?"

"Not yet. Now the game begins again but with bigger stakes."

"What do you...?" But Talia didn't finish her question. The tingling at the back of her neck gave her the answer. Jean Luc was close by.

"No, Chris. This is between us!"

"Not anymore. Not when you involved him. Is he your lover, Talia?"

"Why do you care? You left me for dead thirty years ago."

Jean Luc burst through the door. He looked from Chris, to Annie, and finally to Talia. "What is happening here?"

Chris pushed Annie away, and she frowned at the abrupt gesture. "Glad to see you could make it."

"You called and told me Renato was here. Where is he?" He glanced at Talia. "Why are you here?"

"Yes, tell him Talia, why you are here."

Not like this. "He is my..." She couldn't say it. She choked on the word.

"Sire." Chris finished for her. "She is mine, Jean Luc. I made her."

Jean Luc flinched as if he had been slapped. His eyes narrowed and turned red and he growled. Low and hoarse. A growl full of fury and promise of retribution.

He took a step toward Chris.

"Ah, ah, ah, my friend. Remember your oath." Chris grinned.

Oh, God. "No, Chris!"

Jean Luc glanced at her, eyes flaring in surprise. "Chris?"

"That was the name I was using thirty years ago. When I met Talia."

"You knew him before he turned you?"

Chris laughed out loud. "This is fabulous! You told him you didn't know me?"

"I didn't know you were a vampire. I didn't know you would turn me against my will."

Jean Luc went deathly still and stared at her, his jaw clenched, and his claws extended.

Talia's claws extended, and she dug them into the palms of her hands. Now he would hate her forever. Now he would leave her alone. If she survived.

CHAPTER 16

Jean Luc forced himself to breathe slowly. His world was incinerating around him. Talia and Leo? Why had she not told him the truth? Had she been playing him the fool? And Leo. What had he become?

He looked at Annie, who stood beside Leo, taking the scene in like a bystander at a traffic accident. Her fresh scent had changed altogether into a spicy mixture of ginger that gagged him with its intensity. Was nothing real anymore?

Leo stepped around the bar. "Your oath is actually why I brought you here today. Talia has threatened me. So I invoke the oath, Jean Luc. You will protect me or die trying."

Talia shook her head, tears streaming down her cheeks. "Don't do this. Let him go."

"What has happened to you, Leo?" Jean Luc asked.

"Don't look at me like that. As though I disgust you. We are the same, you and I. Both turned to do a vampire's bidding, and then what? We have spent centuries living by rules created to keep us in line. I was a soldier, Jean Luc. I was to live and die fighting, and then I was turned."

"So you kill and turn people against their will?"

"I take the rights that should have been ours in the first place!"

"And what of this game with Renato?"

"Renato is a puppet. He always has been. He thinks he will be the next leader? He needs to think again. I am next in line, if he falls. And he will fall, and I will be a founding vampire and eventually leader of the vampires."

Jean Luc grimaced. "You have become LeBlanc. He was everything we swore to destroy. And now he stands reincarnated in front of me."

"No! Never speak his name to me!"

Jean Luc stepped closer, clenching his fists. "You forced Talia to become a vampire!"

Leo's eyes glazed over. "She was my first. I had to have her. And after I turned her, I knew there was no going back. I shouldn't have left her that day, but I panicked. I had taken that forbidden step." He stared at Talia. "You were the most beautiful woman I had ever seen. Still are." Then he turned to Jean Luc with a twisted grin. "And she was amazing in bed. Is she still a back-scratcher? She was such a treat to fuck."

An inhuman screech bounced off the walls and around the room as Annie charged at Leo, sword in hand. Jean Luc stepped in front of him, his body forcing him to protect. Fire pierced his shoulder as her sword connected.

Talia screamed.

Annie lunged again and swung the sword. Jean Luc pivoted. Crimson ran down his arm. He elbowed Annie in the face and grabbed the sword as it fell from her hands. He spun, using the momentum to take off her head in a clean sweep.

Her body crumpled to the floor.

Leo shrugged. "She was getting too clingy anyway." He smiled. "Now kill Talia."

"No."

"What do you mean, no?"

Jean Luc stood taller even though the pain urged him to crumple to the floor. "The oath is a life for a life. I just saved you. We are even now." He tossed the sword to Talia, who caught it with ease.

Leo grinned. "You would let a fledgling fight me?"

"It is her fight."

"You would watch me kill her?"

Jean Luc flashed his fangs. "I will watch her wreak vengeance."

Talia held the sword in her hands and advanced. Leo reached behind the bar and grabbed another sword.

"We need to make this a fair fight."

Talia advanced on him. "Since when have you ever played fair?"

He shook his head. "I didn't think you had it in you to kill your sire."

"You bled me dry, Chris. But you're not my sire. A sire is someone who stands by you and teaches you what it means to be a vampire."

They circled each other, Leo with a cocky swagger, Talia with cautious, feline steps. After a few more seconds, Leo swung the sword, and Talia blocked it easily.

Leo's eyes widened. "You have been practicing."

Leo flashed, and Talia flashed with him. Metal clanged, sparks appearing in the air where they fought. Jean Luc tried to flash as well so he could see what was happening, but he could not make his body obey.

Leo slowed first and stood panting with blood running down his arm. Talia appeared next, and she did not appear to be hurt. Leo bellowed, charging her. She ducked out of the way, and he surged past her. She turned and swung down with a ferocious shout, connecting with his neck. The cut was clean.

Jean Luc fell to his knees. The adrenaline that had kept him on his feet had vanished.

Talia's sword clattered to the floor, and she knelt beside him, holding him up.

"You let me kill him."

"I was not in any shape to challenge him."

"How did you know I would win?"

"Because he underestimated you. You are amazing, Talia. Never let anyone tell you otherwise."

"I'm so sorry, Jean Luc."

He nodded, and his eyes closed. Everything would be all right now.

When he awoke, he was in a bed at the BSR facility. Talia was gone. He did not even attempt to stretch his senses to find her. His heart told him she was not there.

Kyle and Misha sat by his bed, and they both stood and smiled when they saw he was awake.

"It is about time you woke up, my friend." Misha glanced at Kyle and she cleared her throat.

"Jean Luc…"

"I know. She has left."

"She gave you blood and stayed here until Doc told her you were healing, then she left. I'm sorry."

"It will be fine, Kyle."

Kyle rushed on. "She's scared and pushed you away to protect you. Don't let her get away with it."

"I do not plan to."

Misha smiled. "You are going after her, yes?"

"*Oui.*" Talia had left him again. But this time he would not let her go.

CHAPTER 17

Jean Luc walked around tombstones and across the grass to reach the open grave. A priest stood with his hand on the casket, head bent forward in silent prayer. After a couple of seconds, he lifted his head and then shook the lone mourner's hand before turning toward his car.

Jean Luc stepped up to the grave. "I thought I might find you here."

Talia stared at the casket for a moment and then placed a single white rose on its bare top. "I couldn't let Melanie be buried alone."

"I understand." And he did. He reached for her hand.

She stepped away from him. "Don't."

"Don't what? Comfort you?"

She blew out a hard breath. "Comfort me? I don't need comfort. I didn't even know her."

"But you empathize with her. Or is it more than that? Do you see yourself in her?"

"I don't know what you're talking about." She strode away from the grave toward a newer area of the cemetery with no headstones.

Jean Luc walked up behind her. "Talia."

"What?" she snapped, continuing to stare across the grass.

"You do not have to be alone like Melanie. Do not follow her path."

She whirled to face him. "What the hell do you mean?"

"I don't know what happened to Melanie to make her turn away from everyone. Caused her to believe money and blood could give her what she needed in this life, but she did. And nothing can change that. But you have a choice."

A tear rolled down her cheek. "Why are you here, Jean Luc? What do you want?"

And there was that question again. They had come full circle, only this time he knew how to answer it.

"You. I want you, Talia."

She shook her head. "How can you say that? I lied to you about Chris. Have been lying to you for thirty years. And you still want me?"

"I will always want you."

Talia's eyes glistened, and she blinked rapidly. "But...I pushed you away. I didn't want you to fight my battles, to die for me...and you almost died anyway."

He grabbed her shoulders. "*Femme stupide!*"

Gold shot through her pupils, and she glared at him. *Bien!* This was the Talia he was used to seeing.

"Did you just call me stupid?"

"*Oui.* You were willing to die for me. Yet you do not allow me the same choice? I would die for Misha and Kyle. They are my family."

"And what am I?"

He cupped her face with his hands. "You are *mon coeur.* If you were to cease to exist, so would I. Of course I would die for you."

Tears coursed down her cheeks, and he rubbed them away lightly with his thumbs.

"*Je t'aime*, Talia Walker."

She hesitated, and then whispered, "I love you too."

He leaned in and lightly brushed his lips over hers, savoring her flavor. He backed up to gauge her reaction. Her eyes sparked with heat.

He grasped her hand, and they walked toward the parking area. It was time to leave the cemetery and the past behind. "We need to talk about the future. Do you wish to stay in Las Vegas?"

Her eyes widened in shock. "You would come here with me? You would leave Kyle and Misha?"

"If you need to stay here, yes."

"I'll miss Will. But no, your home is with your family. Do you think they'll be okay with me being there after everything that happened?"

"Misha...is Misha. Of course, he wants you to come to Cleveland. And Kyle told me not to return without you."

Talia came to a stop. "Wait. I have to know. Why does she have your mark?"

"Last summer Sebastian decided he wanted Kyle as his own. He would do anything to have her, including biting her against her will to place her under his thrall. He wanted to control Kyle's gift."

Her eyes widened in understanding. "So you bit her to stop him. And you two have never..."

"*Non!* She is like a daughter to me." He shook his head. "I cannot believe she was right."

"About what?"

"Kyle told me you were angry when you saw her bite mark."

"I wasn't angry."

"Jealous?"

"You cocky vamp!"

He grinned and nestled her against him. "*Oui,* but

only when I see the truth with my own two eyes."

Talia locked her arms around him. "We need to talk to Nicholas."

Jean Luc pulled back a bit to look into her face. "I already did. I told him I would quit if he tried to keep us apart."

"And what about the vampire tribunal?"

"When I informed Nicholas of the case, I told him about the founding vampires, and he warned Tobias. Tobias has gone on the offensive. He has attacked Renato's credibility, asking why he allowed Leo to set him up as a killer. The others have pulled back for now."

"You have been busy." She smiled up into his face.

And it was *the* smile. The brilliant smile she had used to greet Misha. And it was just for him. Finally.

His phone buzzed in his pocket, and he groaned at the interruption. "I know who this is." He eased back to pull it out, and Misha's name flashed on the screen. "If I do not answer, he will keep calling every five minutes."

Talia laughed, and the glorious sound sent warmth rushing through to his bones.

"Answer it."

He hit the speaker button. "Hello, Misha."

"Jean Luc, what's going on? Have you seen Talia yet?"

"Yes." He winked at her.

"And? Please tell me you didn't screw it up again, vampire," Kyle's voice chimed in. Of course, they would call him together.

Talia stroked her hand across Jean Luc's shoulder and down his arm, taking his hand as she spoke. "He didn't screw it up again. I hope you have room for one more on your team."

The phone went silent for a second and then voices erupted.

"Hot damn!" Kyle yelled.

"Thank God!" Misha gushed.

"When are you coming home?" Kyle and Misha chorused.

Jean Luc laughed.

"Holy shit. He just laughed. Did you hear him *laugh*?" Kyle blurted.

Misha's belly laugh rang loud and clear. "It is music to my ears, my friend."

Jean Luc wrapped his arm around Talia and pulled her to his side again. "I will stay here with Talia until she can move to Cleveland."

"Okay," Kyle replied. "But I want to hear all about what you said to Talia. Did you say what I told you to say, or did you improvise?"

Talia chuckled, and he squeezed her shoulder.

"Sorry, Kyle, but you are breaking up. I have to go now. Talk to you soon."

"Are you giving me the brush-off, Jean Luc? You're in so much trouble when you get—"

He hit the red button on his phone and then, just to be safe, powered it off.

Talia shook her head. "I thought Misha was bad enough all by himself, but with Kyle in the mix? They are going to take some getting used to."

He quirked his eyebrow at her. "They were actually quite well behaved just now."

"Well, I'm up for the challenge," she said, resting her head on his shoulder.

He turned her toward him and cuddled her to his chest. "As am I, *mon coeur*. As am I."

THANKS!

I hope you enjoyed the fourth book in my Mind Sweeper Series. My fifth book is a novel about Kyle and her continuing story. You can find my other books listed on the next page.

And if you are so inclined, please review this book as well.

If you would like to know when my books will be released, please join my new releases email list at www.aejonesauthor.com or follow me on Twitter @aejonesauthor or Facebook at www.facebook.com/aejones.author1.

Mind Sweeper Series

Mind Sweeper
Book 1

The Fledgling
Book 2 (A Mind Sweeper Novella)

Shifter Wars
Book 3

The Pursuit
Book 4 (A Mind Sweeper Novella)

Sentinel Lost
Book 5 (Coming 2015)

If you turn the page, you can read a teaser for *Sentinel Lost*, book five in the series.

Excerpt from

SENTINEL LOST

AE Jones

Chapter 1

"*Knock, knock.*"

"Stop it, Marie," I groaned pulling the comforter up tight around my neck and snuggling further into my bed.

"*Knock, knock.*"

"I'm not answering you."

Marie's head appeared through my closed bedroom door. "I can do this all night you know. Since I'm dead I don't have to be anywhere, anytime soon. *Knock, knock.*"

"Fine. What's there?"

"Don't you mean who?"

"Not in my world."

"You're no fun," Marie huffed and floated the rest of the way through the bedroom door and over to the bed. "I've been spending time with Groucho Marx and thought I'd try out some jokes he taught me."

"Why are you here?"

"I want to know what's going on with Jean Luc and that new vampire."

"That new vampire's name is Talia and she and Jean Luc are finally together after wasting too much time being stupid. I'm just happy Jean Luc actually listened to me."

Marie frowned. "And I'm mad about that, young lady."

"Did you honestly think you were going to have a relationship with my teammate? You're dead and he's a vampire."

"Exactly! He's a vampire, which means he wouldn't be judgmental about me being a ghost."

"You're not corporeal, Marie. How exactly would this have worked?"

"Love finds a way, dear."

I flung my arm over my eyes hoping she would take the hint and go away. "Don't the angels have any control over you? Isn't there a heavenly curfew or something? Marie, it's way too late for this. You need to give me some privacy."

"I give you plenty of privacy when you're playing with your kitty cat."

I growled and moved my arm to glare at her. "Stop calling Griffin that. He's the head of the US shifter contingent, not my kitty cat."

Marie's eyes twinkled. "Whatever you say, dear. Where has he been lately, by the way?"

"In Europe meeting with international shifter leaders."

"Why didn't you go with him?"

"Because it would have been boring and they sure wouldn't have let me attend the meeting."

"Right, we don't need you causing any international incidents."

"Funny."

Marie giggled. "I am, aren't I? Now let me try out

some of these jokes."

My phone rang, *thank God*, and I made a grab for it not checking to see who it was. Even if it was a telemarketer I was happy for the save. "Sorry, but I have to get this. Hello."

"Kyle, are you still up?"

I glared at Marie some more and she smiled back at me. "Yes, Misha, I'm awake. What's up?"

"Just got a call from the PD. Priority. The captain wants to meet with us, in person."

I sat up. "Shit, that can't be a good sign. Do you have any idea what's going on?"

"No, little one. Jean Luc and I will be there in five minutes."

"I'll be ready."

I flung back the comforter and scrambled out of bed. "I've got a call, Marie. Some supe messed up and as usual we've got to cover it up. Can't talk anymore about Jean Luc. Now go away so that I can get dressed."

"Kyle, sweetie, we have the same lady parts."

"Marie!"

She chuckled and faded away. I dressed quickly in jeans and a turtleneck. I pulled on thick socks and one of my boots before hopping on one foot out into my hall while I yanked on the other one. Then I hopped right through Marie who was floating in front of me. Icy pinpricks skittered over my skin.

"Holy crap! I thought you left." I frowned. "Are you haunting me? Do I need to burn something of yours to set you free?"

"What in the world are you talking about?"

"Well, unless you're tied to me for some strange reason, I can't figure out why you would spend your undead days in Cleveland, Ohio."

Marie smiled. "It's not the place that attracts me, dear. It's the people. Now your teammate, Misha, is a Shamat demon right?"

Warning bells sounded in my head. "Yes."

"Is he single?"

"We are so not going there."

"Russians are a very passionate people."

I shuddered. "It's official. I'm going to need therapy."

Tires squealed outside and I ran over to my window and looked down at the street below. The team van sat in front of my apartment building, smoke still rising from the tire burns on the street. One of these days, my neighbors were going to call the cops on Jean Luc. "See you later!"

I grabbed my coat, hustled down the stairs, and hopped into the back of the van. "Thank God for late night calls."

Jean Luc peeled away from the curb. "Rough night, *ma petite*?"

"You could say that."

ABOUT THE AUTHOR

Growing up a TV junkie, award winning author AE Jones oftentimes rewrote endings of episodes in her head when she didn't like the outcome. She immersed herself in sci-fi and soap operas. But when *Buffy* hit the little screen, she knew her true love was paranormal. Now she spends her nights weaving stories about all variation of supernatural—their angst and their humor. After all, life is about both...whether you sport fangs or not.

AE lives in Ohio with her eclectic family and friends who in no way resemble any characters in her books. *Honest.* Now her two cats are another story altogether.

25100392R00069

Made in the USA
San Bernardino, CA
17 October 2015